MAIGRET TESTIFIES:

I was busy signing letters, your honor, and that took time. Eventually, I looked up and said, reproachfully, "That was not a very nice thing to do, Meurant. Why did you lie to me?"

Meurant's ears reddened. His lips moved.

"Until now," I went on, "I didn't think you could have been guilty, not even suspected of it. But what can you expect now that I know you went to the Rue Manuel on February 27th? What did you go there for? Why did you keep quiet about it?"

Then Meurant lowered his head and mumbled, "I am innocent, sir. They were already dead."

MAIGRET
IN COURT

GEORGES SIMENON

Translated from the French
by Robert Brain

AVON BOOKS · NEW YORK

AVON BOOKS
A division of
The Hearst Corporation
105 Madison Avenue
New York, New York 10016

First Avon Books Printing: June 1988

AVON TRADEMARK REG. U.S. PAT. OFF. AND IN OTHER COUNTRIES. MARCA
REGISTRADA. HECHO EN U.S.A.

Printed in the U.S.A.

K–R   10   9   8   7   6   5   4   3   2   1

To Denise

One

Had he been there two hundred times? three hundred times? or even more? He had no desire to count them, or to recall each individual case, even the most famous of them, those that had found a place in legal history, since this was the most unpleasant part of his profession.

Yet did not most of his investigations lead in the end to the assize, or criminal, court, like today, or to the police court? He would have preferred not to know about it, at least to keep out of these last rites, to which he had never altogether become habituated.

In his office on Quai des Orfèvres, the conflict, which most often was not decided until the small hours of the morning, was still a battle of one man against another, more or less on equal terms.

Go along a few corridors, a few staircases, and it was a different setting, another world, where words no longer held the same meaning, an abstract, hieratical universe, pompous and preposterous at the same time.

With other witnesses, he had just left the court-room, with its solemn paneling, where the light from the electric bulbs mingled with the grayness of a rainy afternoon. The attendant, whom Maigret would

1

have sworn had always looked as old as he did now, led them to a smaller room, like a schoolmaster leading his pupils, and gestured to the benches fastened to the walls.

Most of them went and sat down obediently and, respecting the judge's instructions, did not utter a word, even hesitated to look at their companions.

They looked straight in front of them, tense, withdrawn, saving their secrets until that solemn moment when, quite soon now, alone in the center of an awesome space, they would be questioned.

It was rather like being in the sacristy. As a little boy, when he had gone each morning to serve Mass at the village church, Maigret used to feel a similar nervousness as he waited to follow the priest toward the altar, lit by flickering candles. He could hear the footsteps of the unseen faithful going to their pews, the sacristan walking up and down.

In the same way, now he was able to follow the ritual ceremony that was being performed beyond the door. He could recognize the voice of Judge Bernerie, the most meticulous, the fussiest of magistrates, but also perhaps the most scrupulous and the most passionate seeker of the truth. Thin and in poor health, with a dry cough, his eyes feverish, he resembled a saint in a stained-glass window.

Then came the voice of Aillevard, the procurator, who sat on the public prosecutor's bench.

Finally steps approached, those of the court attendant, who opened the door a crack and called:

"Detective Inspector Segré."

Segré, who had not sat down, glanced across at Maigret and went into the courtroom, in his overcoat, a gray hat in his hand. The eyes of the rest followed him for a moment, thinking that it would be their turn soon and anxiously wondering how they would acquit themselves.

A small patch of colorless sky was visible through some inaccessible windows, placed so high up that they were opened or closed only with the help of a cord, and the electric light sculpted the faces beneath with blank eyes.

It was warm, but it would not have been proper to take his overcoat off. There was this ritual, to which everyone on the other side of the door paid strict attention, and it made no difference that Maigret came only from next door, along the corridors of the gloomy Law Courts: he wore an overcoat like the rest, and carried his hat in his hand.

It was October. The chief inspector had returned only two days ago from his vacation, to a Paris drowning in apparently interminable rain. Back on Boulevard Richard-Lenoir, then in his office, he would have found his feelings hard to define; there was certainly as much pleasure as sadness in coming home.

In a short while, when the judge asked him his age, he would answer:

"Fifty-three."

And that meant that, according to regulations, he would be retired in two years' time.

He had often thought about it and often looked forward to it. But this time, on his return from his vacation, retirement was no longer a vague or distant prospect; it was a logical conclusion, ineluctable, practically immediate.

Their future, during the three weeks they had spent on the Loire, had begun to materialize when the Maigrets finally bought the house where they would spend their declining days.

It had happened almost against their will. As in previous years, they had stayed at a hotel in Meung-sur-Loire, where they had formed their own habits, and the landlord and his wife, the Fayets, treated them as members of the family.

Signs on the walls of the little town announced the sale by auction of a house at the edge of the fields. They went to see it, he and Madame Maigret. It was a very old building, which, with its garden surrounded by a gray wall, reminded them of a rectory.

They had been captivated by the blue-flagstoned hallways, the kitchen, with its huge beams, three steps down from ground level, which still had its pump in one corner. The living room smelled like the parlor of a convent, and throughout the house the windows, with their tiny panes, mysteriously dissected the sun's rays.

At the sale the Maigrets, standing at the back of the room, had received several curious looks, and people had been surprised when the chief inspector had raised his hand, while the villagers turned around to look. . . . Going . . . Going . . . Gone!

For the first time in their lives they were property owners, and, the very next day, they arranged for the plumber and the carpenter to call.

During the last few days they had even begun to tour the local antique shops. They had bought, among other things, a wooden chest with the coat of arms of Francis I, which they had placed in the downstairs hall, near the living-room door, where there was a stone mantelpiece.

Maigret had not mentioned anything about it to Janvier, or to Lucas, not to a soul, rather as if he were ashamed to be planning his future in this way, as if it were a treasonable offense in respect of the Quai des Orfèvres.

The previous day, his office had no longer looked quite the same to him, and this morning, in the witnesses' room, listening to the echoes from the courtroom, he was beginning to feel like a stranger.

In two years' time he would be going fishing, and probably playing *belote* on winter afternoons with a few cronies in a corner of a café where he had already begun to go regularly.

Judge Bernerie was asking precise questions, which the inspector from the Ninth Arrondissement was answering with no less precision.

The witnesses on the benches around Maigret, men and women, had all passed through his office, and some of them had spent several hours in it. Was it because they were overwhelmed by the solemn atmosphere of the place that they seemed not to recognize him?

It was not he who would question them this time, it was true. They would not be appearing, this time, before a man like themselves, but in front of an impersonal machine, and it was even uncertain whether they would understand the questions that would be put to them.

The door half opened. It was his turn. Like his colleague from the Ninth Arrondissement he held his hat in his hand, and without looking to left or right he walked up to the semicircular balustrade of the witnesses' stand.

"Your last name, first name, age, and profession . . ."

"Maigret, Jules, fifty-three, divisional chief inspector at Police Headquarters, Paris."

"You are neither related to nor employed by the accused . . . ? Raise your right hand. . . . Swear to tell the truth, nothing but the truth . . ."

"I swear. . . ."

He saw, on his right, the members of the jury, their faces standing out more clearly than others in the halflight, and on the left, behind the black gowns of the lawyers, the accused man, sitting between two uniformed guards, his chin on his clasped hands, staring intently at him.

They had spent long hours alone, the two of them, in the overheated office on Quai des Orfèvres, and they had sometimes broken off the interrogation to eat sandwiches and drink some beer, chatting like old friends.

"Listen, Meurant . . ."

Perhaps Maigret had occasionally used *tu* to him?

Here, an insurmountable barrier separated them, and Gaston Meurant's look was as noncommittal as the chief inspector's.

Judge Bernerie and Maigret were also acquainted, not only because they had chatted together in the corridors, but because this was the thirtieth time the one had been interrogated by the other.

It had left no trace. Each played his part as if they were strangers, officiating in a ceremony as ancient and ritualistic as the Mass.

"It was you, Divisional Chief Inspector, who conducted the investigations into the facts of which the court has now been apprised?"

"Yes, your honor."

"Please turn to the members of the jury and tell them all you know."

"Last February 28th, at about one o'clock in the afternoon, I was in my office on Quai des Orfèvres when I received a telephone call from the duty officer of the Ninth Arrondissement. He informed me that a crime had just been discovered on Rue Manuel, not far from the Rue des Martyrs, and that he was on his way to the scene. A few minutes later I had a call from the public prosecutor's department asking me to go along as well and to send forensic and laboratory experts there."

Maigret heard a few coughs behind him, shoes scraping on the floor. It was the first case of this court session, and all the seats were occupied. There were probably spectators standing at the back, near the big door guarded by uniformed policemen.

Judge Bernerie belonged to that minority of magistrates who, applying the penal code to the letter of the law, do not content themselves with hearing a summary in the courtroom of the examining magistrate's findings, but go over it all again in its smallest details.

"You found the public prosecutor's staff on the premises?"

"I arrived several minutes before his deputy. I found Inspector Segré with his assistant and two detectives from the district. Nothing whatever had been touched by any of them."

"Tell us what you saw."

"Rue Manuel is a quiet street, middle-class, with little activity in it, and it runs into the bottom of Rue des Martyrs. The house, number 27a, is situated almost halfway along the street. The concierge's lodge is not on the ground floor, but on the one above. The inspector, who was waiting for me, took me up to the second floor, where I saw two doors opening off the landing. The one on the right was ajar, and on a small copper plaque was the name Madame Faverges."

Maigret was aware that for Judge Bernerie every point counted, and that he must omit nothing or he would be dryly called to order.

"In the hall, lit by an electric lamp with frosted glass, I noticed no disorder."

"One moment, please! Were there, on the door, any signs of its having been forced?"

"No. Experts examined it later. The lock has been removed. It has been established that no instrument of the type generally used to force locks was employed on it."

"Thank you. Please proceed."

"The apartment consists of four rooms, apart from the entrance hall. Opposite the front door is a living room; the glass door to the room has cream curtains. It was in this room, which leads through another glass door into the dining room, that I saw the two bodies."

"Where were they exactly?"

"That of the woman, who I afterward learned was named Léontine Faverges, was lying on the carpet, her head turned toward the window. Her throat had been cut by means of some weapon which was no longer in the room, and on the carpet there was a pool of blood more than twenty inches across. As for the child's body . . .''

"You mean the young Cécile Perrin, the four-year-old girl who normally lived with Léontine Faverges?''

"Yes, your honor. The body was curled up on a Louis Quinze sofa, her face buried beneath some silk cushions. According to the local doctor, and shortly afterward Dr. Paul as well, after an attempt to strangle her, the child was smothered by those cushions. . . .''

A murmur ran through the room, but the judge had only to raise his head, run his eyes along the rows of spectators, for silence to reign again.

"After the appearance of the members of the public prosecutor's department, you stayed on in the apartment with your colleagues until evening?''

"Yes, your honor.''

"Tell us what conclusions you reached.''

Maigret hesitated only a few seconds.

"From the first, I was struck by the furnishings and the interior decoration. According to her papers, Léontine Faverges had no profession. She had a small private income and looked after Cécile Perrin, whose mother, a nightclub entertainer, could not do so herself.''

The mother, Juliette Perrin, he had noticed as he entered the room, was seated in the front row of the body of the court, since she was claiming damages. Her hair was dyed red and she was wearing a fur coat.

"Tell us exactly what surprised you about the apartment.''

"An unusual elegance, a special style which reminded me of certain apartments in the days before the laws on prostitution. The living room, for example, was overpadded, overripe, with a profusion of rugs, cushions, and sentimental prints on the walls. The blinds were of delicate shades, as they were also in the two bedrooms, which had more mirrors than one might ordinarily expect. I gathered, in due course, that Léontine Faverges had indeed formerly kept her apartment as a place of assignation. After the new laws were passed, she carried on for a while. The Vice Squad had to get after her, and she gave up and stopped all activity only after being fined several times."

"Were you able to discover what financial resources she had?"

"According to the concierge, women who lived nearby, and everybody who knew her, she had put money aside, since she had never been a spendthrift. Her maiden name was Meurant; a sister of the accused's mother, she arrived in Paris when she was eighteen and worked for a time as a saleswoman in a department store. At twenty she married a man named Faverges, a traveling salesman, who died three years later in a car accident. The couple were then living in Asnières. For several years the young woman was seen frequenting the cafés on Rue Royale, and the Vice Squad had a record of her."

Have you made inquiries, among people she knew at that time, for anyone who might have remembered her recently and decided to attack her?"

"She was a solitary person, apparently, something rather unusual for her kind. She saved her money, which enabled her, later on, to set herself up on Rue Manuel.''

"She was sixty-two years of age when she died?''

"Yes. She had grown fat, but as far as I could judge, she had retained a kind of youthful appearance and a coquettish way about her. According to the witnesses I questioned, she was very attached to the little girl, whom she boarded less for the slight income it procured her, it seems, than for fear of loneliness.''

"Did she have a bank account?''

"No. She had no faith in loan societies, trustees, or investments of any sort, and kept everything she had at home.''

"Was the money found?''

"Very little—some change, some notes of small denomination in a handbag, and some more change in a kitchen drawer.''

"Was there a hiding place and did you discover it?''

"Apparently there was. Whenever Léontine Faverges fell ill, which happened two or three times over the last few years, the concierge would go up to do her housework and look after the child. On a chest of drawers in the living room there was a Chinese vase with a bunch of artificial flowers in it. One day the concierge wanted to dust the flowers, so she took them out of the vase. She found in the bottom a linen purse, which she thought contained gold pieces. From its size and weight the concierge says there must have been more than a thousand. A test was carried out in my office with a linen bag and a thousand pieces. It was apparently conclusive. I questioned the staffs of various banks in the neighborhood. At a branch of the Crédit Lyonnais they remembered a woman, whose description corresponded to that of Léontine Faverges, who they said bought bearer bonds at various times. One of the cashiers, named Durat, officially recognized her from a photograph.''

"So it is likely that these bonds, like the gold pieces, would have been in the apartment somewhere. But you did not discover anything?''

"No, your honor. We naturally searched for fingerprints on the Chinese vase, on the drawers, and more or less all over the apartment.''

"With no result?''

"Only the fingerprints of the two residents and, in the kitchen, those of a delivery boy whose movements have been checked. His last delivery was on the morning of the 27th. And, according to Dr. Paul, who performed the autopsy on both bodies, the crime was not committed earlier than the evening of February 27th between five and eight o'clock.''

"Have you questioned all the occupants of the building?''

"Yes, your honor. They confirmed what the concierge had already told me; in other words, that Léontine Faverges had no men visitors apart from her two nephews.''

"You mean the accused, Gaston Meurant, and his brother, Alfred?''

"According to the concierge, Gaston Meurant came to see her fairly regularly, once or twice a month, and his last visit had occurred about three weeks before. As for his brother, Alfred Meurant, he put in only rare appearances at Rue Manuel, because he was not in his aunt's favor. By questioning her neighbor across the hall, Madame Solange Lorris, a dressmaker, I learned that a customer of hers had come to see her for a fitting on February 27th, at about half past five. This person is named Madame Ernie and lives on Rue Saint-Georges. She states that just as she was going up the stairs, a man came out of the dead woman's apartment, and that when he saw her, he seemed to change his mind. Instead of going downstairs, he went up toward the third floor. She was unable to see his face clearly, because the staircase is badly lighted. According to her, the man was wearing a navy suit and a chestnut-colored belted raincoat.

"Tell us how you first got in touch with the accused."

"While my men and I were examining the apartment on the afternoon of February 28th, and were starting to question the other tenants, the evening papers came out with news of the crime and printed a certain number of details."

"One moment. How was the crime discovered?"

"About noon that day—I mean February 28th—the concierge was surprised not to have seen either Léontine Faverges, or the little girl, who usually attended a kindergarten nearby. She went and rang the bell. Receiving no answer, she went up again a little later, still without result, and eventually she telephoned the police. But to get back to Gaston Meurant, the concierge knew only that he was a picture-framer and that he lived near Père-Lachaise. I had no need to start a search for him, because the next morning . . ."

"That's March 1st . . ."

"Yes. The next morning, as I was saying, he turned up of his own accord at the Ninth Arrondissement police station saying that he was the murdered woman's nephew, and the station sent him along to me. . . ."

Judge Bernerie was not one of those judges who took notes, or during a hearing deal with their correspondence. Still less did he doze off, and his eyes darted incessantly from the witness to the accused, with an occasional brief glance at the jury.

"Tell the court as exactly as possible about this first interview you had with Gaston Meurant."

"He was wearing a gray suit and a fairly old fawn raincoat. He seemed slightly overawed at being in my office, and I got the impression that it was his wife who had persuaded him to pay that visit."

"Did she accompany him?"

"She stayed outside in the waiting room. One of my inspectors came and informed me she was there, so I asked her to come in. Meurant told me he had read the newspapers, that Léontine Faverges was his aunt, and that, because he believed that he and his brother were the only near relatives the murdered woman had, he thought he had better make himself known. I asked him how he got on with the old lady, and he replied that they got on very well together. Still in answer to my queries, he added that his last visit to Rue Manuel had been on January 23rd. He was unable to give me his brother's address since he no longer kept in touch with him."

"So, on March 1st the accused categorically denied that he was at Rue Manuel on February 27th, the day of the crime.

"Yes, your honor. Asked about his movements, he told me that he had been working, in his workshop on Rue de la Roquette, until half past six that evening. I visited this workshop in due course, and the store as well. The store has only a rather narrow window and is crammed with frames and engravings. A suction bracket, on the back of the glass door, is used to hang a notice that reads: 'If not here apply at the end of the courtyard.' An unlighted passageway leads down, and there at the end is the workshop where Meurant constructed his picture frames."

"Is there a concierge?"

"No. The house has only two upper floors, which you reach by a staircase leading off the yard. It is a very old building squeezed in between two tenements."

One of the assistant judges, whom Maigret did not know, since he had recently arrived from the country, was staring straight ahead of him at the public with an air of not hearing a thing. The other, on the contrary, rosy-cheeked, white-haired, was nodding his head approvingly at Maigret's every sentence, some of which, God knows why, drew a smile of contentment from him. As for the jury, they stayed as still as if, for example, they were the painted plaster figures around a Christmas crèche.

Counsel for the defense, Pierre Duché, was a young man, and this was his first important case. Nervous, seeming always about to jump to his feet, he bent over his files from time to time, covering them with notes.

Meurant alone showed, it might have been thought, a complete lack of interest in anything that was going on around him, or, more exactly, was watching this performance as if it were no concern of his.

He was a man of thirty-eight, relatively tall, broad-shouldered, with curly reddish-blond hair, blue eyes, and the complexion that often goes with red hair.

All the witnesses described him as a gentle, mild-mannered person, not very gregarious, whose life was divided between his workshop on Rue de la Roquette and his apartment on Boulevard de Charonne, through the windows of which one could see the tombstones of Père-Lachaise cemetery.

He was a pretty fair representative of the solitary craftsman type, and the one thing surprising about him was the wife he had chosen.

Ginette Meurant was petite, with an excellent figure; she had that look about her, that way of pouting her lips, that kind of body which make one automatically think of sex.

Eleven years younger than her husband, she seemed even younger, and she had the childlike habit of fluttering her eyelashes as if she did not understand.

"How did the accused account for his movements between five o'clock and eight o'clock on February 27th?"

"He told me that he had left his workshop at about half past six, turned out the store lights, and gone home on foot, as he usually did. His wife was not in the apartment. She had gone to the movies, to the five o'clock show, which was quite a common habit of hers. We have the box office's evidence to this effect. It was a theater on Faubourg Saint-Antoine where she regularly goes. When she got back, a little before eight o'clock, her husband had laid the table and prepared the evening meal."

"Was this usual?"

"Apparently."

"The concierge at Boulevard de Charonne saw her tenant come in?"

"She doesn't remember. There are about twenty apartments in the building, and at the end of the afternoon people are coming in and going out pretty frequently."

"Did you mention the vase, the gold pieces, and the bearer bonds to the accused?"

"Not that day, but the next, March 2nd, when I summoned him to my office. I had only just then heard about that money, from the concierge on Rue Manuel."

"Did the accused appear to know about it?"

"After some hesitation he eventually admitted that he did."

"His aunt had taken him into her confidence?"

"Indirectly. I shall have to launch into a digression here. About five years ago, Gaston Meurant, apparently at his wife's prompting, gave up his trade to buy a café-restaurant property on Rue du Chemin-Vert."

"Why do you say 'at his wife's prompting'?"

"Because when Meurant first met her, eight years ago, she was a waitress in a restaurant on Faubourg Saint-Antoine. It was through eating there that Meurant got to know her. He married her and, according to her, insisted that she stop working. Meurant admits this too. Ginette Meurant's ambition was nevertheless to be the proprietress of a café-restaurant someday, and when the opportunity arose, she persuaded her husband. . . ."

"Things went badly for them?"

"Yes. Within the first few months Meurant was

forced to approach his aunt and borrow money from her.''

"Did she lend him any?''

"Several times. According to her nephew, there was, in the Chinese vase, besides the bag of gold pieces, an old wallet containing bank notes. The sums she handed over to him were taken from this wallet. She used to laugh and call the vase her Chinese safe.''

"Have you traced the accused's brother, Alfred Meurant?''

"I hadn't done so then. I simply knew from our files that he lived an irregular sort of existence and that he had twice been convicted for procuring.''

"Have witnesses stated that they saw the accused in his workshop on the afternoon of the crime, after five o'clock?''

"Not at that time.''

"Was he wearing a blue suit and a chestnut raincoat, according to his statement?''

"No. His everyday suit, which is gray, and a light fawn raincoat which he generally puts on to go to work.''

"If I understand you correctly, there was no precise piece of evidence enabling you to charge him?''

"That is correct.''

"Can you tell us what direction your investigations took during the days following the crime?''

"First of all, the past life of the murdered woman, Léontine Faverges, and the men she had known. We were also interested in the activities of the child's mother, Juliette Perrin, who, being aware of the contents of the Chinese vase, might have mentioned it to friends.''

"These inquiries produced nothing new?"

"No. We questioned everyone living on the street as well, and all those who might have seen the murderer walk past."

"Without result?"

"Without result."

"So that, on the morning of March 6th, your investigations had still got nowhere?"

"That is correct."

"What happened on the morning of March 6th?"

"I was in my office at about ten o'clock when I received a telephone call."

"Who was it from?"

"I don't know. The caller was unwilling to give his name, and I motioned to Inspector Janvier, who was standing beside me, to try to trace the call."

"Was he successful?"

"No. The conversation was too brief. I only recognized the characteristic click of a telephone-booth phone."

"Was it a man or a woman who spoke to you?"

"A man. I'd have sworn that he was speaking through a handkerchief to disguise his voice."

"What did he say to you?"

"His actual words were: 'If you want to trace the Rue Manuel murderer, ask Meurant to show you his blue suit. You'll find bloodstains on it.' "

"What did you do?"

"I went along to the examining magistrate, who provided me with a search warrant. Accompanied by Inspector Janvier, I reached Boulevard de Charonne at ten past eleven, and on the third floor I rang the bell of the Meurants' apartment. Madame Meurant opened the door. She was in her dressing gown, wearing slippers. She told us her husband was at his workshop, and I asked her if he owned a navy-blue suit.

" 'Yes,' she answered. 'His Sunday suit.'

"I asked to see it. The apartment is comfortable, stylish, with a cheerful look about it, but even at that time of day it was still untidy.

" 'Why do you want to see this suit?'

" 'Just a simple verification . . .'

"I followed her into the bedroom, where she took a navy-blue suit from the closet. Then I showed her the search warrant. The suit was packed away in a special bag I had brought, and Inspector Janvier filled in the usual receipts.

"Half an hour later the suit was in the hands of laboratory experts. During the course of the afternoon I was informed that it did in fact bear bloodstains on the right sleeve and on the lapel, but I had to wait until the next day before I knew if it was human blood. From noon, however, I arranged for a discreet watch to be kept on Gaston Meurant and his wife.

"The next morning, March 7th, two of my men, Inspectors Janvier and Lapointe, armed with a warrant for arrest, presented themselves at the workshop on Rue de la Roquette and proceeded to arrest Gaston Meurant.

"He seemed surprised. He said, without resisting:

" 'There must be some misunderstanding.'

"I was waiting for him in my office. His wife, in another office nearby, seemed more upset than he was."

"Are you able, without the help of notes, to repeat, as closely as possible, the interview you had with the accused that day?"

"I think I can, your honor. I was sitting at my desk and I had left him standing. Inspector Janvier was standing beside him; Inspector Lapointe was sitting ready to take down the interrogation in shorthand.

"I was busy signing letters, and that took some time. Eventually I looked up and said, reproachfully:

" 'That was not a very nice thing to do, Meurant. Why did you lie to me?'

"His ears reddened. His lips moved.

" 'Until now,' I went on, 'I didn't think you could have been guilty, not even suspected of it. But what can you expect now that I know you went to Rue Manuel on February 27th? What did you go there for? Why did you keep quiet about it?' "

The judge was leaning forward so as to miss nothing of what would follow.

"What was his answer?"

"He mumbled, his head lowered:

" 'I am innocent. They were already dead.' "

Two

The judge must have made a discreet sign beckoning the court attendant, who moved quietly around behind the bench and leaned over him, while Duché, the young counsel for the defense, pale and tense, tried to guess what was going on.

The judge uttered a few words only, and everyone in the room followed his gaze as he stared up at the windows, placed high in the walls, with cords hanging from them.

The radiators were scorching. An invisible steam, smelling increasingly of human bodies, rose from the hundreds of people, pressed elbow to elbow, from their damp clothes, their breathing.

The attendant, moving like a sacristan, made his way toward one of the cords, tried to open a window. It wouldn't budge. He tugged three times more, and everyone waited in suspense, their eyes following his every movement; there was eventually a nervous laugh when he decided to try the next window.

This incident made people aware of the external world once more, seeing trickles of rain on the windowpanes, clouds beyond, hearing all at once more distinctly the sound of braking cars and buses.

At this very moment, as if to punctuate the pause, there even came the noise of an ambulance or police-car siren.

Maigret was waiting, worried, concentrating. He had taken advantage of the respite to glance across at Meurant, and, as their eyes met, he thought he read a look of reproach in the blue eyes of the prisoner.

Not for the first time, at this same bar, the chief inspector was feeling a kind of despondency. In his office on Quai des Orfèvres, he was still in touch with reality, and even when he was composing his report he could believe that his sentences adhered to the truth.

Then months would pass, sometimes a year, if not two, before he found himself one fine day shut up in the witnesses' room with the people he had questioned ages ago, who were now no more than a memory to him. Were they really the same human beings—concierges, passers-by, shopkeepers—who now sat there, staring vacantly, on the sacristylike benches?

Was it the same man, after months in prison, now in the dock?

They had suddenly been plunged into a depersonalized world where everyday phrases seemed no longer to be current, where the most commonplace actions were translated into cut-and-dried formulas. The judges' black robes, the ermine, the red gown of the solicitor general further increased this feeling of some ceremony with changeless ritual, where the individual counted for nothing.

Judge Bernerie, however, conducted the proceedings with the maximum of patience and humanity.

He never pestered the witnesses to finish, never interrupted them when they seemed bogged down in useless detail.

Other magistrates, more rigorous, often made Maigret clench his fists with anger and powerlessness.

Even today he knew he was giving only a lifeless, sketchy semblance of reality. Everything he had just said was true, but he had not been able to convey the weight of things, their density, their tiniest stirrings, the smell of them.

It seemed to him indispensable, for example, that those who were about to sit in judgment on Gaston Meurant should be made to perceive the atmosphere of the Boulevard de Charonne apartment as it was when he had first found it.

His description, in two sentences, was of no earthly use. He had been struck, from the start, by the couple's living quarters, in that huge building full of households and children, overlooking the cemetery.

Whose ideas had been imposed on the rooms, their decoration, their furnishing? In the bedroom, instead of a proper bed there was one of those three-cornered couches, surrounded by shelves of the kind called "cozy corners." It was covered in orange satin.

Maigret tried to imagine the picture frames, the craftsman busy all day in his workshop, at the end of a courtyard, returning from work and coming home to this setting that recalled those in magazines: the lighting almost as subdued as on Rue Manuel, the furniture too fragile, too stylish, the pastel colors . . .

Nevertheless, the books on the shelves certainly belonged to Meurant, nothing but volumes bought secondhand from bookshops or the embankment stalls:

Tolstoy's *War and Peace;* eighteen bound volumes
of *The History of the Consulate and the Empire,* in
an old edition which already smelled of musty paper;
Madame Bovary; a work devoted to wild animals,
and, next to it, *History of the Religions of the
World. . . .*

Here was clearly a believer in self-education. In
the same room were piles of sentimental newspapers,
glossy magazines, movie reviews, romantic novels,
all obviously constituting Ginette Meurant's fare, like
the records, near the phonograph, which bore the
titles of popular songs.

How did they spend the evenings, she and he, and
all day Sunday? What words did they exchange?
What were their activities?

Maigret also realized he had not given an exact
idea of Léontine Faverges, or of her apartment, where
gentlemen with families and reputations used once to
pay discreet visits and where, in order to prevent
their meeting each other, they were whisked out of
sight behind heavy curtains.

"I am innocent. They were already dead. . . ."

In the courtroom, packed like a movie theater, that
sounded like a desperate lie, since the public, which
was acquainted with the case only through the
newspapers, and probably the jury too, looked on
Gaston Meurant as a murderer who had not hesitated
to put to death a little girl, first trying to strangle her
and then, nervous because she would not die quickly
enough, suffocating her beneath silk cushions.

It was barely eleven o'clock in the morning, but
had these people here any notion now of the time, or
even of their own private lives? Among the jury

members there was a bird seller from Quai de la
Mégisserie and a plumber who had a little business in
which he worked himself with two helpers.

Was there also someone here who had been married to a woman like Ginette Meurant, and whose
reading matter, in the evenings, was similar to that of
the accused?

"Please continue, Chief Inspector."

"I asked him to give me an exact account of his
movements on the afternoon of February 27th. At
two o'clock, as usual, he opened his store and hung
up the sign behind the door to ask people to call at
the workshop. He went through to it and worked on
several flames. At four o'clock he turned on the
lights and went back to the store to light up the
window. According to him still, he was in his workshop when, shortly after six o'clock, he heard steps
in the courtyard. Somebody tapped on the window.

"It was an old man, whom he says he had never
seen before. He was looking for a flat decorated
frame, about sixteen inches by twenty-two, for an
Italian gouache he had just bought. Meurant says he
showed him frames in various sizes. After asking
about the price, the old man is then said to have
left."

"Has this witness been found?"

"Yes, your honor. Only three weeks afterward.
He is named Germain Lombras, a piano teacher, who
lives on Rue Picpus."

"Have you questioned him personally?"

"Yes, your honor. He states that he did indeed go
to Meurant's workshop a little after six o'clock one
evening. He had happened to walk past the shop the

very day after he had bought a Neapolitan landscape from an antique shop.''

''Did he tell you what the accused was wearing?''

''Apparently Meurant was wearing gray trousers under an unbleached work smock and had taken his tie off.''

Aillevard, the procurator, in the public prosecutor's seat, who was following Maigret's testimony in a file he had, was about to ask permission to speak when the chief inspector hastened to add:

''The witness found it impossible to state exactly whether this scene took place on Tuesday or Wednesday; that's to say, on February 26th or 27th.''

Now it was defending counsel's turn to become agitated. The young lawyer, for whom everyone was predicting a brilliant future, was virtually staking it on this case. At all costs, he had to give the impression of a man sure both of himself and of the cause he was defending, and he was trying very hard to keep his hands still and not let them betray him.

Maigret went on, his voice impersonal:

''The accused claims that after this visit he shut up the workshop, then the store, before going off in the direction of the bus stop.''

''Which would place his departure at about six-thirty?''

''Near enough. He got off the bus at the bottom of Rue des Martyrs and made his way to Rue Manuel.''

''Did he have any special reason for visiting his aunt?''

''At first he told me he hadn't, that it was just an ordinary visit, such as he was in the habit of making at least once a month. Two days later, however, when we learned about the unhonored bill of exchange, he went back on his statement."

"Tell us about this bill of exchange."

"On the 28th, Meurant was due to honor a fairly substantial bill of exchange. He did not possess the necessary funds."

"Was this bill of exchange presented?"

"Yes."

"Was it met?"

"No."

The solicitor general gestured, as if to sweep away this argument in Meurant's favor, while Pierre Duché turned to the jury with the air of calling them to witness.

The fact had worried Maigret, too. If the accused, after cutting his aunt's throat and suffocating little Cécile Perrin, had taken away the gold pieces and the notes hidden in the Chinese vase, if he had appropriated the bearer bonds as well, at a time when he was still not under suspicion and might well think he never would be, why had he not met the bill and avoided the risk of being declared bankrupt?

"My detectives have calculated the time it takes to get from Rue de la Roquette to Rue Manuel. By bus you would have to reckon about half an hour at that time of day, and by taxi you need twenty minutes. Inquiries among taxi drivers have led to nothing; as have those among bus conductors. Nobody remembers seeing Meurant.

"According to his subsequent statements, which he has signed, he arrived at Rue Manuel a few minutes before seven. He met nobody on the stairs, did not see the concierge. He knocked on his aunt's door, was surprised, after getting no answer, to see the key in the lock.

"He went in and found the scene previously described."

"Were the lights on?"

"The main floor lamp in the living room, with its salmon-pink shade, was on. Meurant thinks there were lights on in other rooms, but it is simply an impression he got, because he did not enter them."

"How does he explain his behavior? Why didn't he take the trouble to call a doctor, to warn the police. . . ?"

"For fear of being accused. He noticed a drawer in the Louis Quinze desk open and he shut it. In the same way he put back in the Chinese vase the artificial flowers, which were lying on the floor. As he was about to leave he realized that through what he had done he had probably left fingerprints, and he wiped the piece of furniture, then the vase, with his handkerchief. He also wiped the door handle, and, finally, before going down the stairs, he took the key with him."

"What did he do with it?"

"He threw it down a drain."

"How did he get home?"

"By bus. The route for Boulevard de Charonne runs through quieter streets, and apparently he was in his apartment by twenty-five to eight."

"His wife wasn't there?"

"No. As I said, she had gone to a local movie for the five o'clock show. She went to the movies a lot, nearly every day. Five box-office girls remembered her on seeing her photograph. While he waited for

her, Meurant started reheating the leftovers from a
roast and some string beans, then set the table."

"Was that a common occurrence?"

"Quite common."

He had the feeling, even with his back to the
public, that everybody, especially among the women,
was smiling.

"How many times have you interrogated the
accused?"

"Five times; one time for eleven hours. Once his
statements were no longer inconsistent, I wrote out
my report, which I handed to the examining magistrate, and since then I've had no opportunity of seeing
him again."

"He didn't write to you, when he was in prison?"

"Yes, he did. The letter has been entered in the
file. He affirms, once again, that he is innocent and
asks me to look after his wife."

Maigret noticed Meurant make a slight movement
and avoided meeting his eye.

"He didn't tell you what he meant by that, or what
he was afraid of on her account?"

"No, your honor."

"Did you find his brother?"

"Two weeks after the crime on Rue Manuel; on
March 14th, to be precise."

"In Paris?"

"At Toulon, where, although he does not reside
there permanently, he spends most of his time, with
frequent trips along the Riviera, sometimes to Marseilles, sometimes to Nice and Menton. He was first
examined by the Toulon police, on a rogatory com-
mission. Then, when summoned to my office, he

duly came, but not without insisting that his traveling expenses should be paid in advance. According to him, he hadn't set foot in Paris since January, and he gave us the names of three witnesses with whom he played cards, at Bandol, on February 27th. The witnesses have been heard. They belong to the same sort of world as Alfred Meurant; the underworld, as you might put it.''

''What was the date when you submitted your report to the examining magistrate?''

''The final report, together with the various statements signed by the accused, was delivered on March 28th.''

They were reaching the tricky moment. Only three of them were aware of it, among those playing major roles. First the procurator, Justin Aillevard, whom Maigret had visited in the public prosecutor's office at five o'clock the day before. Then, apart from the chief inspector himself, Judge Bernerie, who had also been informed the day before, later in the evening, by the solicitor general.

But there were others, unsuspected by the general public, who were also awaiting this moment: five detectives Maigret had chosen from among those less well known, some who belonged to that part of the Vice Squad generally known as the Society Section.

Since the opening of the trial they had been in the courtroom, scattered among the crowd at strategic points, watching the faces, keeping an eye on the reactions.

''Officially, therefore, Chief Inspector, your investigations came to an end on March 28th.''

''That's right.''

"Nevertheless, have you, since that date, concerned yourself with the actions and movements of persons closely or distantly connected with the accused?"

At once counsel for the defense rose, ready to protest. He was probably about to point out that it was not in order to admit further evidence, against his client, which had not been entered in the depositions.

"Please be calm, Counsel," the judge said to him. "You will see in a moment that if I am using my discretionary powers to admit an unexpected development in this case, it is not with the intent to damage the prisoner's cause."

The solicitor general, for his part, looked across at the young defense lawyer somewhat ironically, rather as if to protect him.

"I repeat my question. Did Chief Inspector Maigret, after all, continue his investigations unofficially?"

"Yes, your honor."

"On your own?"

"With the consent of the director of Police Headquarters."

"You kept the public prosecutor's office informed?"

"Not until yesterday, your honor."

"Did the examining magistrate know that you were continuing to be concerned in the case?"

"I did mention it to him in passing."

"You were not, however, acting on his instructions, or on those of the attorney general?"

"No, your honor."

"It is essential that this should be clearly established. That is why I have referred to this, in some

ways, complementary investigation as an unofficial
one. What was your motive, Chief Inspector, in continuing to employ your detectives on inquiries which
the transfer of the case to the grand jury of the assize
court rendered no longer necessary?''

The quality of the silence in the room had changed.
Not the slightest cough could now be heard, not a
single shoe shifted on the floor.

''I was not satisfied with the results obtained,''
Maigret growled in a surly voice.

He couldn't say what he most deeply felt. The
verb ''to satisfy'' only partly expressed his thoughts.
The facts, to his mind, did not fit with the characters.
How could he explain this in the solemn setting of
the court, where they expected precise sentences from
him?

The judge was just as experienced in criminal
cases as himself—more, in fact. Each evening he
took back files to peruse in his apartment on Boulevard Saint-Germain, where the light in his study
often remained on until two o'clock in the morning.

He had seen men and women of all sorts pass in
and out of the dock and the witness box.

Yet weren't his contacts with life always theoreti-
cal? He had not himself been in the workshop on Rue
de la Roquette, or into the odd apartment on Boulevard de la Charonne. He did not know the swarming
life that went on in those buildings, or in the crowded
streets, the bistros, the local dance halls.

Prisoners were brought before him between two
policemen, and all he knew about them he had found
in the pages of a file.

Facts. Sentences. Words. But all around them—what of that?

His assistant judges were in the same position. The solicitor general as well. The very dignity of their functions isolated them from the rest of the world, in which they formed a little island apart.

Among the members of the jury, among the spectators, there were probably some who were better equipped to understand the character of a Meurant, but these people were not qualified to express their views or knew nothing of the complicated apparatus of the law.

Was Maigret not, himself, on both sides of the fence at the same time?

"Before allowing you to continue, Chief Inspector, I would like you to tell us the result of the analysis of the bloodstains. I am referring to those that were discovered on the blue suit belonging to the defendant."

"It was human blood. Minute laboratory tests later showed that this blood and that of the victim possess a sufficient number of similar characteristics for it to be scientifically certain that they were from one and the same body."

"In spite of that you proceeded with your investigation?"

"Partly because of that, your honor."

The young lawyer, who had prepared to dispute Maigret's statement, could not believe his ears, remained restless, while the chief inspector went steadily rumbling on.

"The witness who saw a man in a blue suit and a chestnut raincoat leave Léontine Faverges's apartment about five o'clock is positive about the time. The time has been checked, besides, by a shopkeeper in the neighborhood on whom this person called before going to her dressmaker on Rue Manuel. If one accepts Lombras's testimony, although he is less definite about the date of his visit to Rue de la Roquette, the accused was still in his workshop, wearing his gray trousers, at six o'clock. We have calculated the time necessary to get from that workshop to Boulevard de la Charonne, then the time needed to change and finally go to Rue Manuel. It takes, at the lowest estimate, fifty-five minutes. The fact that the bill of exchange, which fell due the next day, was not met also struck a wrong note with me.''

"So you turned your attention to Alfred Meurant, the prisoner's brother?''

"Yes, your honor. At the same time, my colleagues and I started other inquiries.''

"Before allowing you to give us the result of them, I must be certain that they are strictly connected with the present case.''

"They are, your honor. For several weeks, detectives from the Hotels Section showed certain photographs around a large number of Paris rooming houses.''

"What photographs?''

"Alfred Meurant's, first. Then one of Ginette Meurant.''

It was the prisoner who leaped to his feet this time, indignant, and his counsel had to rise in turn to calm him and force him to sit down again.

"Give us your conclusions as briefly as possible.''

"Alfred Meurant, the prisoner's brother, is well

known in certain districts, particularly around Place
des Ternes and the neighborhood of Porte Saint-
Denis. We found his registration cards at a small
hotel on Rue de l'Etoile, among others, where he has
often stayed, but there is nothing to show that he has
been in Paris since January 1st.

"Finally, although he has been seen around with
numerous women, nobody remembers meeting him
in his sister-in-law's company, at least during a
period that goes back more than two years."

Maigret sensed Meurant looking at him hostilely;
the man had clenched both his fists, and his lawyer
was continually glancing around at him for fear of an
outburst.

"Please continue."

"Ginette Meurant's photograph was recognized
immediately, not only by the staffs of the movie theaters, particularly the local theaters, but also at the
dance halls both around La Chapelle and on Rue de
Lappe. She has frequented these places for many
years, always in the afternoon, and the last dance hall
she has attended to date is one on Rue des Gravilliers."

"Did she go to them alone?"

"She has had a certain number of boy friends at
them, never for long. However, during the last few
months before the murder, she was not seen often."

Didn't all this evidence explain the atmosphere on
Boulevard de Charonne, the magazines and records,
their contrast with the books Meurant went to buy
from secondhand booksellers?

"When I left for my vacation, a little less than a
month ago now," Maigret went on, "the various

departments of Police Headquarters had discovered nothing further.''

"During this case has Madame Meurant been under surveillance by the police?"

"Not constant surveillance, in the sense that she was not followed every time she went out, and there was not always a detective outside her door at night."

Laughter in the courtroom. A sharp look from the judge. Silence once again. Maigret wiped his brow, embarrassed by the hat he still held in his hand.

"Was this surveillance, even though sporadic," the judge was asking, not without irony, "the result of the letter the prisoner sent you from prison and was it intended to protect his wife?"

"I wouldn't say that."

"You were trying, if I understand you correctly, to discover her habits and contacts?"

"First of all, I wanted to know whether she ever met her brother-in-law in secret. Then, since I obtained no positive results, I wondered whom she went around with and what she did with her time."

"Chief Inspector, you questioned Ginette Meurant at Police Headquarters. She stated to you, if I remember correctly, that she returned home on February 27th at about eight o'clock in the evening and found dinner ready to be served. Did she tell you which suit her husband was wearing?"

"Gray trousers. He had no jacket on."

"And when he left her after lunch?"

"He was in a gray suit."

"At what time did she herself leave the apartment on Boulevard de Charonne?"

"About four o'clock."

"So that Meurant might have come and changed afterward, gone out, changed again when he returned, without her knowing?"

"It's physically possible."

"Let's return to the subsequent investigations you embarked upon."

"Following Ginette Meurant revealed nothing. After her husband's imprisonment, she stayed at home most of the time, going out only to do her shopping, to visit the prison, and two or three times a week to go to the movies. The surveillance, as I have said, was not continuous. Its results only confirm what we have been told by neighbors and shopkeepers. The day before yesterday, I returned from my vacation and found a report on my desk. It might be just as well to explain that the police never completely lose touch with a case, so that sometimes an arrest is made, fortuitously, two or three years after a crime or an offense."

"In other words, during the past months, no further *systematic* investigations of the actions and movements of Ginette Meurant were carried out?"

"That's correct. Detectives from the Hotels Section and the Vice Squad, as well as my own detectives, always carried her photograph in their pockets, however, as well as one of her brother-in-law. They would show them around from time to time. It was in this way that, on September 26th, a witness recognized one of his regular clients in the photograph of the young woman."

Meurant grew excited again, and it was the judge's turn, this time, to give him a stern look. From the body of the court someone was protesting, probably Ginette Meurant.

"This witness is Nicolas Cajou, manager of a small hotel on Rue Victor-Massé, around the corner from Place Pigalle. He is normally in the office of his place, and through the glass door he can keep an eye on people going in and out."

"Wasn't he questioned last March or April, like other hotel proprietors?"

"He was in the hospital at that time for an operation, and his sister-in-law was there in his place. Subsequently, he spent three months convalescing in the Morvan, where his family come from, and it was not until the end of September that a man from the Hotels Section, just by chance, showed him the photograph."

"Ginette Meurant's photograph?"

"Yes. He recognized her at first glance, saying that, up until he left for the hospital, she used to come there with a man he did not know. One of the chambermaids, Geneviève Lavancher, also recognized the photograph."

At the press table the reporters looked at each other, then turned to the judge in surprise.

"I suppose the companion you alluded to is not Alfred Meurant?"

"No, your honor. Yesterday, in my office, where I asked Nicolas Cajou and the chambermaid to come, I showed them several hundred identification pictures in order to be satisfied that Ginette Meurant's companion is not in our records. The man is short, thickset, with very dark brown hair. He dresses carefully and wears a ring with a yellow stone. He is said to be about thirty years old and he smoked American cigarettes, which he chain-smokes, so that after each of his visits to Rue Victor-Massé the ashtray was always piled with butts, only a few of which had lipstick on them.

"I haven't had the requisite time, before the trial, to undertake a thorough investigation. Nicolas Cajou went into the hospital on February 26th. On the 25th he was still in his office in the hotel, and he states that the couple paid a visit that day."

There was a stir in the courtroom, unseen by Maigret, and the judge raised his voice, something he did very rarely, and pronounced:

"Silence, or I shall clear the court."

A woman's voice tried to make itself heard:

"Your honor, I . . ."

"Silence!"

As for the prisoner, his jaw tightly set, he was looking at Maigret with hatred.

Three

Nobody stirred while the judge leaned across toward each of his assistants in turn and spoke to them in undertones. A three-way colloquy took place, which again recalled a religious rite, since one could see their lips moving noiselessly as if for responses, their heads nodding in a curious rhythm. At one stage the solicitor general, in his red robe, left his seat to put in his own words, and a little later it seemed as if the young counsel for the defense was about to follow his example. He was visibly hesitating, worried, not yet quite sure of himself, and he was almost on his feet when Judge Bernerie rapped on the bench with his gavel and each magistrate resumed his position, as in a tableau.

Xavier Bernerie announced, in a low voice:

"The court thanks the witness for his testimony and asks him not to leave the courtroom."

Still like an officiating priest, he felt around for his cap, donned it, and, rising to his feet, concluded his recital:

"The hearing is adjourned for a quarter of an hour."

The next second there was a din as of school being

let out, almost an explosion, scarcely muffled at all, of sounds of all sorts jumbled together. Half the spectators left their seats; some were standing in the aisles, gesticulating; others were jostling each other in an attempt to reach the main door, which the police had just opened, while the guards whisked away the prisoner through an exit hardly distinguishable from the paneling of the walls. Pierre Duché had difficulty following him, and the jurors, on the other side, also disappeared behind the scene.

Lawyers in gowns, most of them young, including a woman who might have been a cover girl on a magazine, formed a black-and-white cluster by the witnesses' entrance. They were discussing articles 310, 311, 312, and so on in the code of criminal procedure, and some of them were talking excitedly of irregularities in the conduct of the hearings, which would inevitably lead to an appeal.

An elderly lawyer with yellow teeth, in a shiny gown, an unlit cigarette hanging from his lower lip, was calmly invoking precedents, citing two cases, one at Limoges in 1885, the other at Poitiers in 1923, when the preliminary investigation had not only been entirely recast at the public trial, but had take a new turn as a result of unexpected testimony.

Of all this, Maigret, a motionless block, saw only jostling figures, heard only scraps of conversation, and he hadn't had time to locate in the courtroom, where there were now several empty spaces, more than a couple of his men before he was surrounded by reporters.

The same overexcitement reigned as on a first night at the theater, after the first act.

"What do you think about this bombshell you've just dropped, Chief Inspector?"

"What bombshell?"

He was filling his pipe methodically and he felt thirsty.

"You believe Meurant's innocent?"

"I don't believe anything."

"You suspect his wife?"

"Gentlemen, you'll have to forgive me, but I've nothing to add to what I said in the box."

The pack only stopped pestering him, abruptly, when a young reporter suddenly dashed across to Ginette Meurant, who was trying to reach the exit, and the rest were afraid they might miss some sensational statement.

Everybody watched the group move along. Maigret, taking advantage of it to slip through the witnesses' door, came upon men smoking cigarettes in the hallway and others, unfamiliar with the building, looking for the lavatories.

He knew that the magistrates were deliberating in the judge's chamber; he saw an attendant leading young Duché, whom they had sent for, in that direction.

It was almost noon. Bernerie obviously wanted to have the matter cleared up during the morning's hearing in order to resume the ordinary course of the trial that afternoon, hoping for a verdict the same day.

Maigret reached the open hallway, lit his pipe at last, beckoned to Lapointe, whom he saw leaning against a pillar.

He was not the only one wanting to take advantage

of the adjournment to have a glass of beer. Outside, people could be seen running across the street in the rain, with their collars turned up, to dive into the cafés nearby.

At the Law Courts bar an impatient crowd, in a hurry, was disturbing those lawyers and their clients who, a few moments ago, had been quietly discussing their particular business.

"Beer?" he asked Lapointe.

"If you can get any, Chief."

They thrust their way between backs and elbows. Maigret made a sign to a bartender he had known for twenty years, and a few seconds later two nicely foaming glasses of beer were passed to him over the heads of other customers.

"See if you can find out where she has lunch, who with, who she speaks to, and who it is if she phones anyone."

The tide was already ebbing, and people were hurrying to get back to their seats. When the chief inspector arrived at the courtroom, it was too late to reach the rows of benches, and he had to lean against the small door, among the lawyers.

The jury was in its place, the prisoner as well, between his guards, his counsel lower down in front of him. The judges entered and sat down with dignity, probably conscious, like the chief inspector, of the change that had taken place in the atmosphere.

A short time ago they had been here to deal with a man accused of having cut the throat of his aunt, a sixty-two-year-old woman, and having smothered, after attempting to strangle, a little four-year-old girl.

Wasn't it natural that there had been a grim and somewhat stifling sense of seriousness in the air?

Now, after the adjournment, everything was changed. Gaston Meurant had now left the limelight, and even the double crime had lost some of its importance. Maigret's evidence had introduced a new element, posed a new problem, suggestive, shocking, and the whole room now showed no interest in anything except the young woman whom the occupants of the back rows were trying in vain to glimpse.

This alone caused a buzz of noise, and the judge could be seen scanning the crowd sternly, as if he were searching for the troublemakers. This lasted a long time, but as the minutes passed, the noise died down, finally disappeared altogether, and silence reigned again.

"I warn the general public that I shall not tolerate any disturbance, and if there is any incident whatsoever I shall have the court cleared."

He coughed, murmured a few words in the ears of his assistants.

"By virtue of the discretionary powers conferred upon me and in agreement with the counsels for the prosecution and the defense, I have decided to hear three new witnesses. Two are in the courtroom, and the third, the aforesaid Geneviève Lavancher, who has been summoned by telephone, will appear at this afternoon's hearing. Will the attendant call Madame Ginette Meurant."

The old attendant advanced across the empty space to meet the young woman sitting in the front row, who rose, hesitated, then allowed herself to be led to the witness box.

Maigret had talked to her several times at the Quai des Orfèvres. He had then had before him a young woman whose sexiness was vulgar and occasionally aggressive.

In honor of the assize court, she had bought herself a black tailored suit, a skirt with a three-quarter-length jacket; the only touch of color was provided by a straw-colored blouse.

The chief inspector was convinced that it was also to smarten her appearance for the occasion that she was wearing a model hat, which lent a kind of mystery to her face.

She seemed to be playing two roles at the same time, the naïve girl and the smart young wife, lowering her head, raising it to rest timid, docile eyes on the judge.

"Your name is Ginette Meurant, maiden name Chenault?"

"Yes, your honor."

"Speak up and please face the jury. You are twenty-seven years old and were born at Saint-Sauveur in the Nièvre?"

"Yes, your honor."

"You are the wife of the prisoner?"

She replied again in the same good-schoolgirl voice.

"Article 322 precludes your testimony being accepted as evidence, but, with the consent of the prosecution and the defense, the court has the right to hear you for its information."

And, as she was raising her hand in imitation of the previous witnesses, he stopped her.

"No! You do not have to take the oath."

Between other people's heads Maigret caught a glimpse of the pale face of Gaston Meurant staring steadfastly in front of him, his chin resting in his hands. From time to time he clamped his jaws so tightly together that the bones protruded.

His wife avoided turning in his direction, as though that were prohibited, and her eyes were fastened steadily on the judge.

"You knew the murdered woman, Léontine Faverges?"

She seemed to hesitate before murmuring:

"Not very well."

"What do you mean by that?"

"That she and I never visited each other."

"But you had met her?"

"The first time, before our marriage. My fiancé insisted on introducing me to her, saying that she was all the family he had."

"So you have been to Rue Manuel?"

"Yes. One afternoon, about five o'clock. She gave us hot chocolate and cakes. I felt right away that she had taken a dislike to me and that she would urge Gaston not to marry me."

"Why was that?"

She shrugged her shoulders, searched for words, finally spoke out:

"We just weren't the same sort."

A look from the judge halted the laughter that was about to break out.

"She did not attend your wedding?"

"Yes, she did."

"And Alfred Meurant, your brother-in-law?"

"He too. In those days he was living in Paris and was still on good terms with my husband."

"What was his profession then?"

"Traveling salesman."

"He had regular work?"

"How should I know? He gave us a coffee set as a wedding present."

"Did you see Léontine Faverges after that?"

"Four or five times."

"Did she come to your apartment?"

"No. We used to go and see her. I never wanted to go, because I hate imposing on people who dislike me, but Gaston maintained that I couldn't get out of it."

"Why?"

"I don't know."

"Was it, by chance, because of her money?"

"Probably."

"When did you stop going to Rue Manuel?"

"Ages ago."

"Two years? Three years? Four years?"

"About three years, I suppose."

"So you knew about the Chinèse vase that was kept in the living room?"

"I've seen it, and I've even said to Gaston that artificial flowers ought to be kept for funeral wreaths."

"You knew what it contained?"

"Flowers, as far as I was concerned."

"Your husband never said anything to you?"

"What about? The vase?"

"The gold pieces."

For the first time she turned around to the dock.

"No."

"He did not confide in you, either, that his aunt, instead of putting her money in the bank, kept it at home?"

"I don't remember anything about that."

"You can't be sure?"

"Oh, yes . . . Yes . . ."

"During the period when you still paid visits to Rue Manuel, no matter how seldom, was little Cécile Perrin already in the house?"

"I never saw her. No. She would have been too small."

"You've heard about her from your husband?"

"He must have mentioned something about it. Wait a minute! I'm positive now. I remember I was surprised that anybody would let a woman like her look after a baby."

Did you know that the prisoner fairly often went to his aunt to ask for money?"

"He didn't always tell me what he was doing."

"But you knew about it, vaguely?"

"I knew he wasn't much of a businessman, that he could be taken in by anybody, like when we opened a restaurant on Rue du Chemin-Vert, which might have done very nicely."

"What did you do in the restaurant?"

"I waited on the customers."

"And your husband?"

"He worked in the kitchen, with an old woman."

"Did he know about cooking?"

"He used a book."

"Were you the only one in the room with the customers?"

"We had a young waitress at the beginning."

"And when things started going badly, didn't Léontine Faverges help pay off the creditors?"

"I suppose she did. I think we still owe money."

"Did your husband seem worried toward the end of February?"

"He was always worried."

"Did he talk to you about a bill of exchange falling due on the 28th?"

"I didn't notice. There were bills of exchange every month."

"He didn't tell you he would be going to see his aunt to ask for help once again?"

"I don't remember it."

"It wouldn't have struck you?"

"No. I was used to it."

"After the restaurant was closed, you didn't suggest finding a job?"

"I did nothing else. Gaston would not allow it."

"Why not?"

"Because he was jealous probably."

"Did he cause jealous scenes with you?"

"Not scenes."

"Please face the jury."

"I forgot. I'm sorry."

"On what kind of thing do you base your statement that he was a jealous man?"

"First of all, he refused to let me go out to work. Later, on Rue du Chemin-Vert, he kept coming up from the kitchen to spy on me."

"Has he ever followed you?"

Pierre Duché was shifting restlessly on his bench, unable to see what the judge was driving at.

"I haven't noticed that."

"Did he ask you in the evenings where you'd been?"

"Yes."

"What would you reply?"

"That I had been to the movies."

"Are you certain that you never talked to anybody about Rue Manuel or Léontine Faverges?"

"Only to my husband."

"Not to a girl friend?"

"I have no girl friends."

"What people did you and your husband know?"

"Nobody."

If these questions were disconcerting her, she gave no sign of it.

"Do you remember which suit your husband was wearing at lunchtime on February 27th?"

"His gray suit. It was his everyday one. He wore the other one only on Saturday nights, if we went out, and on Sundays."

"And when he visited his aunt?"

"Sometimes he wore his blue suit, I think."

"He did so on that day?"

"I can't say. I wasn't home then."

"You don't know whether he returned to the apartment that afternoon?"

"How could I know that? I was at the movies."

"Thank you."

She was still standing there, bewildered, unable to believe that it was over, that she was not going to be asked the questions everybody was expecting.

"You may go back to your seat."

And the judge continued:

"Will Nicolas Cajou come forward."

There was a feeling of disappointment in the air. The public felt that there had just been some trickery, that a scene had been cut which they had a right to watch. Ginette Meurant sat down again, almost regretfully, and a lawyer standing by Maigret was whispering to his colleagues:

"Lamblin got his claws into her in the hallway during the adjournment. . . ."

The lawyer Lamblin, with a profile like that of a half-starved dog, was a figure who came in for quite a lot of discussion at the Law Courts, rarely favorable, and several times his suspension from the bar had been debated. As if by chance, here he was stationed beside the young woman and he was speaking to her in a low voice, as if congratulating her.

The man who was approaching the witness box, limping, was a completely different specimen of humanity. If Ginette Meurant, underneath all her makeup, had the paleness of women who live in a hothouse atmosphere, this man was not merely pallid but his substance seemed soft and unhealthy.

Had he got so thin as a result of his operation? The fact remained that his clothes, much too big for him, floated around his body, which had lost all its spring and suppleness.

One could better imagine him nestling, in his slippers, in his hotel office, with its frosted windows, than walking along city sidewalks.

He had bags under his eyes, loose skin under his chin.

"You are Nicolas Cajou, sixty-two years old. You were born in Marillac, in the Cantal, and you now keep a hotel in Paris, on Rue Victor-Massé?"

"Yes, your honor."

"You are not related to the prisoner, or a friend of his, or his employee. . . . You swear to tell the truth, the whole truth, nothing but the truth. . . . Raise your right hand. . . . Say: 'I swear . . .' "

"I swear . . ."

One of the assistants leaned toward the judge to make an observation, which must have had some pertinence, for Bernerie seemed to be struck by it, pondered for a good while, finally shrugged his shoulders. Maigret, who had not missed any of this scene, guessed what was going on.

Witnesses who have been convicted, with loss of civil rights, or who indulge in immoral activities are not entitled to be sworn in. Now, was not this hotel-keeper indulging in an immoral practice, since he admitted couples to his establishment under circumstances forbidden by law? Were they sure that his police record carried no convictions?

It was too late to check, and the judge gave a small cough before asking, in an impartial voice:

"Do you normally keep a register of hotel guests?"

"Yes, your honor."

"*All* of them?"

"All those who stay the night."

"But you do not register the names of those who only stop there during the course of the day?"

"No, your honor. The police can tell you that . . ."

That he was a law-abiding citizen, naturally, that there had never been a scandal at his place, and that occasionally he furnished the Hotels Section or Vice Squad detectives with clues they needed.

"Have you looked carefully at the witness who preceded you in the box?"

"Yes, your honor."

"Did you recognize her?"

"Yes, your honor."

"Tell the members of the jury of the circumstances in which you have previously seen this young woman."

"In the usual circumstances."

A look from Bernerie stifled the laughter.

"Which means?"

"Which means that she often appeared in the afternoon in the company of a gentleman who took a room."

"What do you mean by often?"

"Several times a week."

"How many times, would you say?"

"Three or four times."

"Her companion was always the same?"

"Yes, your honor."

"Would you recognize him again?"

"Certainly."

"When did you see him for the last time?"

"The day before I went into the hospital; that's to say, February 25th. I remember the date because of my operation."

"Describe him."

"Not tall . . . Rather short . . . I suspect that, like others who are unfortunately short, he wore special shoes. . . . Always well dresssed, as though he had just stepped out of a bandbox. . . . We know that kind around our way. . . . That's just what surprised me. . . ."

"What do you mean?"

"Because those gentlemen, as a rule, don't make a habit of spending their afternoons in a hotel, especially not with the same woman. . . ."

"I suppose you know all the fauna of Montmartre more or less by sight?"

"Pardon?"

"I mean the men you are talking about. . . ."

"I see them go by."

"However, you have never seen this one except in your hotel?"

"No, your honor."

"And you haven't heard of him before?"

"I only know he's called Pierrot."

"How do you know that?"

"Because the lady who used to come with him sometimes called him that in front of me."

"Did he have any accent?"

"Not strictly speaking. But I always thought that he came from the south, or maybe that he was Corsican."

"Thank you."

This time, again, disappointment was evident on people's faces. They had expected a dramatic identification, and nothing had happened except an apparently innocent exchange of questions and answers.

The judge looked up at the clock.

"The hearing is adjourned and will be resumed at half past two."

The same hubbub as before, with the difference that this time the whole room was emptying and people were forming in two ranks to watch Ginette Meurant pass by. It seemed to Maigret from where he was standing, at some distance, that Lamblin was still following in her wake and that she kept turning around to make sure he was behind her.

The chief inspector had hardly got outside the door when he bumped into Janvier, and looked at him questioningly.

"We've got them, Chief. They're both at the Quai."

It took the chief inspector quite a while to realize that this referred to another case, an armed robbery at a branch bank in the Twentieth Arrondissement.

"How did it happen?"

"Lucas arrested them at the place where the mother of one of the boys lived. The other had been hiding under the bed, and the mother never knew. They hadn't been outside for three days. The poor woman thought her son was ill and kept making him hot toddies. She's the widow of a railwayman and works in a local drugstore."

"How old?"

"The son, eighteen. His pal, twenty."

"They deny it?"

"Yes. But I don't think you'll have much trouble with them."

"What about having lunch with me?"

"I warned my wife I wouldn't be coming home, as it happens."

It was still raining as they crossed Place Dauphine to make their way to the brasserie that had become a kind of annex of Police Headquarters.

"How's it going at the court?"

"Nothing definite yet."

They stopped at the bar while waiting for a table to become vacant.

"I'll have to phone the judge to get his permission not to attend the trial."

Maigret had no wish to spend the afternoon sitting motionless in the crowd, in the humid heat, listening to witnesses who, from now on, would spring no more surprises. He had heard these witnesses, all of them, in the quiet of his office. Most of them he had seen in their homes, in their proper surroundings, as well.

The assize court had always constituted the most unpleasant, most depressing part of his functions, and each time he had the same feeling of misery.

Was not everything distorted there? Not through any fault of the judges, the juries, the witnesses, or on account of the criminal code or procedures, but because human beings were suddenly reduced, if one can so put it, to a few words, a few sentences.

He had sometimes discussed it with his friend Pardon, the local doctor with whom he and his wife had got into the habit of dining once a month.

Once when his office had been full all day, Pardon had displayed a touch of discouragement, almost of bitterness.

"Twenty-eight patients in the afternoon alone! Hardly time to let them sit down, ask them a few questions. What is it you feel? Where does it hurt? How long has it been going on? The others are waiting, staring at the padded door, and wondering if their turn will ever come. Show me your tongue! Take off your clothes! In most cases an hour wouldn't be sufficient to find out everything one should know. Each patient is a separate case, and yet I have to work on the conveyor-belt system. . . ."

Maigret had then told him of the end result of his own work, in other words, the assize court, since most investigations came to their conclusion there.

"Historians," he had remarked, "scholars, devote their entire lives to the study of some figure of the past on whom there already exist numerous works. They go from library to library, from archives to archives, search for the least item of correspondence, in the hope of grasping a little more of the truth. . . .

"For fifty years or more they've been studying Stendhal's letters to get a clearer idea of his character. . . .

"Isn't a crime almost always committed by someone out of the ordinary, in other words, less easy to comprehend than the man in the street? They give me a few weeks, sometimes only a few days, to steep myself in a new atmosphere, to question ten, twenty, fifty people I knew nothing at all about till then, and, if possible, to sift out the true from the false.

"I've been reproached for going to the scene myself instead of sending my detectives. You wouldn't believe it, but it's a miracle that I'm still allowed this privilege!

"The examining magistrate, who continues on from me, has hardly any more scope, and he sees people, detached from their private lives, only in the neutral atmosphere of his office.

"All he has in front of him, in fact, are men already reduced to mere diagrams.

"He also has only a limited time at his disposal. Hounded by the press, by public opinion, his initiative restricted by a maze of regulations, submerged by administrative formalities that occupy most of his time, what is he likely to find out?

"If it is mere disembodied beings who leave his office, what is left for the assizes, and on what basis is the jury going to decide the fate of one or more of their own kind?

"It's no longer a question of months or weeks, scarcely of days. The number of witnesses is reduced to the minimum, as are the questions that are put to them.

"They come and repeat before the court a condensed version, a 'digest,' as people say nowadays, of everything they have said before.

"The case is merely sketched in with a few strokes; the people concerned are no more than outlines, caricatures almost. . . ."

Hadn't he had that feeling once again this morning, even when he was giving his own evidence?

The press would report that he had spoken "at length" and perhaps be surprised at it. With any other judge than Xavier Bernerie, it was true, he would have been allowed only a few minutes to speak, whereas he had stayed in the witness box for almost an hour.

He had done his best to be precise, to communicate a little of what he himself felt to those who listened to him.

He glanced through the stenciled menu and passed it to Janvier.

"I think I'll have the veal. . . ."

A group of detectives was standing at the bar. He noticed two lawyers in the restaurant.

"Did I tell you my wife and I have bought a house?"

"In the country?"

He had promised himself to keep quiet about this, not for the sake of making a mystery of it, but from a scruple of decency because a connection would inevitably be drawn between this purchase and his retirement, which was no longer so far off.

"At Meung-sur-Loire?"

"Yes . . . It's a bit like a rectory . . ."

In two years he would be done with the assize court, except perhaps on the third page of the newspapers. There he would read the testimony of his successor, Chief Inspector . . .

Who would, in fact, succeed him? He had no idea. They were probably starting to discuss it in higher places, but they would obviously avoid mentioning it in his presence.

"What kind of fellows are these two?"

Janvier shrugged his shoulders.

"Just like the rest of them nowadays."

Through the windowpanes Maigret watched the falling rain, the gray parapet along the Seine, the cars sending up a bow wave of dirty water.

"How was the judge?"

"Not so bad."

"What about her?"

"I've put Lapointe on her tracks. She's fallen into the clutches of a pretty shady lawyer, Lamblin. . . ."

"Did she confess to having a lover?"

"She wasn't asked to. Bernerie is cautious."

It was just as well to remember, in fact, that it was

the trial of Gaston Meurant that was taking place at
the assizes, not that of his wife.

"Cajou recognized her?"

"Of course."

"How did the husband take that?"

"I think he would gladly have murdered me at that
moment."

"Will he be acquitted?"

"It's too soon to tell."

Steam rose from the plates, smoke from cigarettes,
and the names of recommended wines were painted
in white on the mirrors around the room.

There was one small wine from the Loire, from
quite near Meung and the house like a rectory.

———————— Four ————————

At two o'clock Maigret, still accompanied by Janvier, climbed the great staircase at the Quai des Orfèvres, which even in summer, on the gayest of mornings, managed to be gloomy and dim. Today a draft of damp air swept around it and the marks of wet shoes on the steps refused to dry.

Even on the first landing they could hear a faint noise from the floor above, then voices, the sound of people going to and fro could be distinguished, a sure sign that the press had been alerted and was there, with photographers and probably television teams, perhaps newsreel men.

A case was finishing or appeared to be finishing at the Law Courts. A fresh one was beginning. At one end there was already a crowd, at the other only the specialists were left.

At the Quai des Orfèvres also, there was a sort of witnesses' room, the glassed-in waiting room known as the glass cage, and the chief inspector paused on his way past to glance in at the six people sitting there under the photographs of policemen who had died in the performance of their duty.

Was it true that all witnesses look alike? The ones

here came from the same walks of life as those at the Law Courts, ordinary folk, modest working-class people. And there were two women among them who stared straight in front of them, their hands on their leather handbags.

The reporters charged toward Maigret, who calmed them with a movement of his hand.

"Take it easy now! Take it easy! Remember, gentlemen, that I am still in the dark about all this and I haven't even seen these boys . . . ."

He pushed open his office door and promised:

"In two or three hours, maybe, if I have some news for you . . ."

He shut the door, said to Janvier:

"Go and see if Lapointe has arrived."

He was resuming the same old habits as before his vacation, almost as much of a ritual for him as was the ceremonial of the assizes for the magistrates. Taking off his coat and hat, he hung them in the closet, where there was an enamel basin in which he could wash his hands. Then he sat down at his desk, fondled his pipes a little before choosing one and filling it.

Janvier returned with Lapointe.

"I'll see your two idiots in a couple of minutes."

And to young Lapointe:

"Well, what did she get up to?"

"All the way along the corridors and down the big staircase she was surrounded by a mob of reporters and photographers, and there were others waiting for her outside. There was even a newsreel truck parked at the curb. As far as I was concerned, I could catch only a glimpse of her face once or twice through the crowd. She seemed frightened and was obviously begging them to leave her in peace.

"Suddenly Lamblin elbowed his way through the crowd, seized hold of her arm, and dragged her to a taxi he had had time to go off and find. He put her in it, and the cab moved off toward Pont Saint-Michel.

"This all happened like a magic trick. Unable to find a taxi myself, I couldn't follow them. However, a few minutes ago, Mace, from *Figaro*, arrived back at the Law Courts. He had been lucky enough to have his car parked nearby, which meant he was able to trail the taxi.

"According to him, Lamblin took Ginette Meurant to a restaurant on Place de l'Odéon which specializes in seafood and bouillabaisse. They lunched there together, taking their time.

"And now everybody's back in their seats in the courtroom and just waiting for court to reconvene."

"Go back there. Give me a ring now and then. I'd like to know whether the chambermaid's evidence provokes any incident. . . ."

Maigret had been able to get in touch with the judge by telephone and had been given permission by him not to waste his time in court that afternoon.

The five detectives who had been planted about the courtroom during the morning had discovered nothing. They had studied the public with the trained eye that practiced judges of facial expression cast over gambling rooms. None of the men present answered to the description furnished by Nicolas Cajou of Ginette Meurant's companion. As for Alfred Meurant, the prisoner's brother, he was not in the courtroom, or in

Paris, as Maigret had now learned from a telephone call to the Toulon Flying Squad.

Apart from Lapointe, who was returning to the next building by way of the internal corridors, two detectives were staying on in the courtroom, just in case.

Maigret called Lucas, who was dealing with the bank robbery.

"I thought I'd better not start questioning them until you'd had a look at them, Chief. I've just arranged it so that the witnesses could catch a glimpse of them as they walked past."

"Did they recognize both of them?"

"Yes. Particularly the one who had lost his mask, of course."

"Bring the younger one in."

His hair was too long, his face pimply, and he looked unhealthy and unwashed.

"Remove his handcuffs. . . ."

The boy shot him a glance of defiance, obviously determined not to fall into the trap he knew was being set for him.

"Leave me alone with him now."

In cases like this, Maigret preferred to remain alone with the suspect, and there was plenty of time, later on, for his statement to be taken down in writing and for him to be made to sign it.

He puffed away gently at his pipe.

"Sit down."

He pushed a pack of cigarettes across to him.

"Do you smoke?"

The boy's hand trembled. At the ends of his long, blunt fingers the nails were bitten away like a child's.

"You've lost your father?"

"It wasn't me!"

"I'm not asking whether it was you or wasn't you who organized this caper. I'm asking whether your father's alive still."

"He's dead."

"How did it happen?"

"In the sanatorium."

"So your mother's supporting you?"

"I've got a job too."

"Doing what?"

"I'm a furniture polisher."

It would take time. Maigret knew from experience that it was better to tackle it slowly.

"How did you get hold of the gun?"

"I don't have a gun."

"Do you want me to call in the witnesses right away? They're waiting outside."

"They're liars, the whole bunch of them."

The telephone was ringing already. It was Lapointe.

"Geneviève Lavancher has given her evidence, Chief. She was asked roughly the same questions as her boss, plus one extra. The judge asked her, in fact, whether she had noticed anything special about the couple's behavior on February 25th, and she replied that she was indeed surprised to see that the bed had not been touched."

"Are the officially scheduled witnesses testifying yet?"

"Yes. Things are really moving fast now. They hardly get a hearing."

It took forty minutes to break the boy's resistance; he finally burst out sobbing.

So he had been the one armed with the gun. There had been three of them, not two, for an accomplice, who had been waiting at the wheel of a stolen car, had apparently planned the holdup and had then cleared off without the others as soon as he heard the cries for help.

Nonetheless, this boy, who was named Virieu, refused to give his name.

"He's older than you?"

"Yes. He's twenty-three and married."

"He's done this sort of thing before, hasn't he?"

"That's what he said."

"I'll have a chat with you again later, after I've heard what your friend has to say for himself."

Virieu was taken away. They brought in Giraucourt, his friend, who also had his handcuffs removed, and the two boys had the opportunity to exchange looks as they passed each other.

"Did he spill the beans?"

"Did you think he'd be able to keep his mouth shut?"

Just routine. The holdup had misfired. No one had been killed, nobody hurt, not even any damage done, except one windowpane.

"Who had the idea of the masks?"

It hadn't been a very original idea in any case. Professional gangsters in Nice had used carnival masks when they robbed a mail truck a few months ago.

"You weren't armed?"

"No."

"Were you the one who called out when the bank teller came to the window: 'Shoot now, you fool . . .'?"

"I don't know what I said. I lost my head. . . ."

"Don't forget that your pal did what you said and pressed the trigger."

"He didn't shoot anyone."

"But that was only because the gun luckily failed to go off. Perhaps there wasn't a round in the thing? Perhaps the gun was defective?"

The bank staff, together with a woman customer, had stood with their hands up. It was ten o'clock in the morning.

"It was you who called out as you went in:

" 'Hands up, everyone against the wall. This is a holdup!'

"Apparently you added:

" 'This is serious.' "

"I said that because a lady started to laugh."

A woman teller of forty-five, who was now waiting in the glass cage with the others, had seized a paperweight and thrown it out the window, calling for help as she did so.

"Have you been convicted before?"

"Once."

"What for?"

"For stealing a camera from a car."

"You know what you'll get this time?"

The young man shrugged his shoulders, trying hard to be brave.

"Five years, my boy. As for your friend, whether his gun was jammed or not, it's quite likely that he won't get away with less than ten years. . . ."

This was true. The third fellow would be found someday or other. The examining magistrate would soon be on the case, and since, this time, there would be no legal recess to hold up the course of justice, in three or four months' time Maigret would again be testifying before the assize court.

"Take him away, Lucas. There's no longer any reason to keep him separated from his friend. Let them gossip away as much as they like. Send in the first witness."

It was only a matter of formalities now, a lot of red tape to be got through. And, according to Lapointe on the telephone, things were moving even more swiftly in the courtroom, where certain of the witnesses, after only about five minutes in the box, found themselves, to their amazement, and somewhat to their disappointment, back in the crowd, trying to find a place for themselves.

At five o'clock Maigret was still working on the bank robbery, and his office, with the lights now on, was filled with smoke.

"The claim for damages is just being heard. Attorney Lioran has made a short statement. In view of the unexpected developments, he is prepared to associate himself in advance with the solicitor general's closing speech."

"And the solicitor general's speaking now?"

"He began about two minutes ago."

"Call me back when he's finished."

Half an hour later, Lapointe phoned in quite a detailed account of this speech. The procurator, Aillevard, had said, in effect:

"We are here to try the prisoner Gaston Meurant, accused of having, on February 27th, cut the throat of his aunt, Léontine Faverges, then suffocating to death a four-year-old girl, Cécile Perrin, whose mother is claiming damages."

The mother, with her hennaed hair, still wearing her fur coat, had cried out loudly and had to be led, shaken by sobbing, from the courtroom.

The solicitor general had continued:

"From the witness box we have heard some unexpected evidence, which we do not need to take into account as far as this case is concerned. The charges brought against the prisoner have not altered and the questions which the jury must answer still remain the same.

"Was it humanly possible for Gaston Meurant to commit this double crime and to steal the life savings of Léontine Faverges?

"It has been established that he was aware of the Chinese vase's secret and that his aunt on several occasions took money from it to give him.

"Had he a sufficient motive?

"The day following the murder, February 28th, a bill of exchange, which he had signed, fell due, and he did not have the necessary funds to meet it, with the result that he was faced with bankruptcy.

"Finally, do we have proof of his presence in the apartment on Rue Manuel that afternoon?

"Six days later there was discovered, in a closet in his apartment on Boulevard de Charonne, a navy-blue suit belonging to him, which bore, on the sleeve and the lapel, spots of blood the origin of which he was at a loss to explain.

"According to the experts, it was human blood, and more likely than not was the blood of Léontine Faverges.

"There remains some evidence that appears to

contradict this, though no aspersion is cast on the witnesses' honesty by my so putting it.

"Madame Ernie, a customer of the victim's neighbor across the hall, saw a man dressed in a navy suit leave Léontine Faverges's apartment at five o'clock that afternoon, and she is almost prepared to swear that this man had very dark hair.

"On the other hand, you have heard a piano teacher, Monsieur Germain Lombras, tell you that at six o'clock that evening he was with the prisoner in his studio off Rue de la Roquette. Monsieur Germain Lombras has nevertheless admitted to us that he has a slight doubt as to the exact date of this visit.

"We have to consider a heinous crime, committed in cold blood by a man who not only attacked a defenseless woman but also did not shrink from murdering a little girl.

"There can therefore be no question of mitigating circumstances, but simply of the supreme penalty.

"It is for the members of the jury to say, in their own hearts and minds, whether they believe Gaston Meurant to be guilty of this double crime."

Maigret, who had at last finished with his would-be gangsters, was resigning himself to opening the door and facing the press.

"Have they confessed?"

He nodded his head.

"Not too much publicity, please, gentlemen. Above all, don't make too much of them! Don't let others, who might be tempted to imitate them, get the impression that these young kids have done something big. They're a wretched pair, believe me . . . .."

He answered the questions briefly, feeling burdened and tired. His mind was still half in the assize court, where it was the turn of the young counsel for the defense to speak.

He felt tempted to push open the glass door that led through to the Law Courts and go and join Lapointe. But what would be the point? He could imagine the defense's final plea, which would begin like a popular novel.

Wouldn't Pierre Duché dig up as much of the past as possible?

A Le Havre family, poor, swarming with children, who had to start fending for themselves as early as possible. At fifteen or sixteen the girls entered into domestic service, or, rather, they left home for Paris, where they were supposed to be entering into service. Had the parents the time or the means to keep an eye on them? They would write once a month, a painful scrawl, with spelling mistakes, sometimes enclosing a modest money order.

Two sisters had left home in this way. First, Léontine Faverges, who had become a salesgirl in a big department store and had married soon afterward.

Hélène, the younger, had worked in a dairy, then in a haberdasher's on Rue d'Hauteville.

The first girl's husband had died. As for the second, she was soon finding her way around the local dance halls.

Had they kept in touch with each other? It was doubtful. When her husband was killed in an accident, Léontine Faverges had begun to hang around the cafés on Rue Royale and the boardinghouses around the Madeleine, before setting herself up on Rue Manuel.

Her sister, Hélène, had had two children, by unknown fathers, and had brought them up as best she could for three years. Then she had been taken off to the hospital for an operation one evening and had never left there alive.

"My client, members of the jury, educated with public assistance . . ."

It was true, and Maigret could have furnished the lawyer with some interesting statistics on this subject, the percentage, for example, of pupils who turned to crime and eventually wound up in the dock in court.

These were the rebels, the ones who had a grudge against society for their humiliating circumstances.

But, contrary to what one might expect, to what the jury probably imagined, they constitute a minority.

No doubt many of the others are also affected in some way. Throughout their lives they suffer from a feeling of inferiority. But, in fact, their reaction to this is to prove to themselves that they are as good as the next man.

They have been taught a trade and they do their best to become first-class workers.

Their ambition is to have a family of their own, a proper, normal family, with children to take out for a walk on Sundays.

And what sweeter revenge than to start a small firm one day, to set themselves up on their own?

Had Pierre Duché thought about it? Was that what he was now telling them, in the courtroom where people's faces were already showing signs of fatigue?

During the long examination Maigret had been through that morning, he had left something out and now he regretted it. The conversation was, of course, all down in the file. But it was only an unimportant detail.

The third time Ginette Meurant had come to his office at Police Headquarters, the chief inspector had asked her incidentally:

"You have never had a child?"

She was apparently not expecting such a question, for she looked surprised.

"Why do you ask me that?"

"I don't know. . . . I just have the feeling that your husband is the sort of man who would want to have children. . . . Am I wrong?"

"No."

"He did hope you would have some?"

"In the beginning, yes."

He had sensed a hesitation, something slightly obscure, and he had delved more deeply:

"You are not able to have them?"

"No."

"He knew this when he married you?"

"No. We had never talked about that."

"When did he find out?"

"After a few months. Since he was always hoping and kept asking me the same question every month, I thought it better to tell him the truth. . . . Not quite the whole truth . . . But the main point . . ."

"Which is?"

"That I was ill, before I met him, and had to have an operation . . ."

It had lasted like that for seven years. Though Meurant had wanted a family, they had remained simply a couple.

He had set up his own business. Later, giving in to his wife's pestering, he had tried a trade other than his own. As one might have expected, it had turned out disastrously. Nevertheless, he had patiently built up his small picture-framing business once more.

This completed the picture for Maigret, who, rightly or wrongly, suddenly began to attach a great deal of importance to this matter of children.

He was not going so far as to maintain that Meurant was innocent. He had seen equally unobtrusive men, as quiet and gentle on the outside, become violent.

Almost always, in such cases, this was because at one time or another they had been hurt deep down, by something.

Meurant, driven by jealousy, was certainly capable of committing a crime of passion. It was also possible that he would have attacked a friend who had humiliated him.

Perhaps even, if his aunt had refused him money, which he urgently needed . . .

Anything was possible, except, so it seemed to the chief inspector, that a man who had so desperately wanted children would slowly suffocate a little four-year-old girl.

"Hello, Chief . . ."

"Yes?"

"He's finished. The judges and the jury have retired. Some people expect they'll be out a long time. Others, though, are convinced the die is already cast."

"How is Meurant?"

"The whole afternoon you might have thought it no longer concerned him. He seemed far away; his eyes were clouded. When his lawyer said something to him, two or three times, he simply shrugged his shoulders. At the end, when the judge asked him if there was any statement he wanted to make, he didn't appear to understand. The question had to be repeated. He simply shook his head.''

"Did he look at his wife at all?''

"Not once.''

"Thank you. Now listen: did you spot Bonfils in the courtroom?''

"Yes. He's keeping close to Ginette Meurant.''

"Go and tell him to make sure he doesn't lose sight of her on the way out. In fact, to make doubly certain that he isn't given the slip, tell him to get Jussieu to help him. One of the two of them can arrange to have a car ready.''

"I understand. I'll give them your instructions.''

"She'll probably go home eventually, and there must be a man permanently outside the building, on Boulevard de Charonne.''

"And what if . . .''

"If Meurant's acquitted, Janvier, whom I'm going to send over, can look after him.''

"Do you think he . . . ?''

"I couldn't say at all, my boy.''

True enough. He had done his best. He was trying to find out the truth, but there was nothing to prove that he had found it, or even part of it.

The investigation had been conducted in March, then at the beginning of April, with many hours of sunshine over Paris, light clouds, a few showers to suddenly dampen the cool mornings.

The other end of the proceedings was now taking

place in an early spell of autumn weather, overcast, with rain, a low spongy sky, gleaming sidewalks.

To kill time, he signed some documents, went to take a look in the duty room, where he gave Janvier some instructions.

"See that you keep me informed, even in the middle of the night."

In spite of his seeming lack of concern, he was tense, suddenly anxious, as if he were blaming himself for having undertaken too heavy a responsibility.

When the telephone rang in his office, he dashed to it.

"All over, Chief!"

He could hear not only Lapointe's voice, but many different noises, quite a hubbub.

"There were four questions, two concerning each of the victims. The answer is no to all four. His lawyer, right now, is trying to lead Meurant through to the clerk's office, in spite of the crowd, which . . ."

Lapointe's voice was lost for a moment in the din.

"I'm sorry, Chief. . . . I grabbed the first telephone I could get at. . . . I'll be at the office as soon as possible. . . ."

Maigret started walking up and down again, stuffing his pipe, changing it for another because that one didn't draw properly, opening and shutting his door again at least three times.

The hallways of Police Headquarters were deserted again, and only a regular, a casual informer, sat waiting in the glass cage.

When Lapointe arrived, there was still an aura of the assize court excitement about him.

"A great many people predicted it, but it was quite

a moment just the same. . . . The whole room stood up. . . . The little girl's mother, who had returned to her seat, fainted and was almost stepped on. . . .''

"Meurant?"

"He didn't seem to understand. He allowed himself to be led away without really knowing what was happening to him. The reporters who were able to get close enough didn't get a word out of him. So they descended on his wife again, with Lamblin playing her bodyguard.

"Immediately after the verdict, she tried to rush across to Meurant, as if to throw her arms around him. . . . He had already turned his back on the courtroom. . . .''

"Where is she?"

"Lamblin led her off to some office or other, near the lawyers' robing room. . . . Jussieu's taking charge of her. . . .''

It was half past six. Police Headquarters was beginning to empty, lights were being turned off.

"I'm going home to dinner."

"What am I supposed to do now?"

"You go home to dinner too, and get some sleep."

"Do you think anything will happen?"

The chief inspector, who was opening his closet to get out his overcoat and hat, simply shrugged his shoulders.

"Do you remember the search?"

"Very well."

"You're sure there was no gun in the apartment?"

"Positive. I'm convinced that Meurant never possessed a gun in his life. He didn't even do military service, because of his eyesight. . . .''

"See you tomorrow, my boy."

"Okay, Chief."

Maigret caught a bus, then walked along past the façades of the houses on Boulevard Richard-Lenoir, his back bent, his collar raised. When he reached the landing on his floor, a door opened, forming a rectangle of warm light and letting smells of cooking drift out.

"Happy?" Madame Maigret asked him.

"Why?"

"Because he's been acquitted."

"How did you know?"

"I just heard it on the radio."

"What else did they say?"

"That his wife was waiting for him at the exit and that they took a taxi and went home."

He ensconced himself in his familiar world, got back into his habits, his slippers.

"Are you very hungry?"

"I don't know. What's for dinner?"

He was thinking of another apartment, where another couple lived, on Boulevard de Charonne. There could be no dinner prepared over there, but probably some ham and cheese in the pantry.

In the street two detectives would be walking up and down in the rain, unless they had found shelter in some doorway.

What would be happening? After living seven months in prison, what would Gaston Meurant have said to his wife? How would he be looking at her? Had he tried to kiss her, place his hand on hers?

Would she swear to him that everything they had said about her was untrue?

Or would she ask his forgiveness, swearing that she loved no one but him?

Would he go back to his store the next day, to his picture-framing workshop at the end of the courtyard?

Maigret was eating mechanically, and Madame Maigret knew this was no time to ask him questions.

The telephone rang.

"Hello. Yes . . . It's me. . . . Vacher? . . . Is Jussieu with you? . . ."

"I'm phoning from a bistro nearby to give you my report. . . . I don't have anything special to tell you, but I guessed you'd like to know. . . ."

"Have they gone home?"

"Yes."

"Alone?"

"Yes. A few minutes later, the lights were switched on on the third floor. I saw shadows passing back and forth behind the curtain. . . ."

"And then?"

"About half an hour later his wife came down, carrying an umbrella. Jussieu followed her. She didn't go far. She went to a delicatessen, next a baker's, then she went back upstairs. . . ."

"Did Jussieu see her close up?"

"Quite close, through the delicatessen window."

"How did she seem?"

"She looked as though she'd been crying. Her cheeks were flushed, her eyes shining. . . ."

"She didn't seem upset?"

"Not according to Jussieu."

"And since then?"

"I suppose they had something to eat. I saw Ginette

Meurant's silhouette again, in the room which seems to be the bedroom. . . ."

"Is that all?"

"Yes. Shall we both stay here?"

"I think it would be wise. I would like one of you to go upstairs and keep watch inside the building in a little while. The tenants probably go to bed early. Perhaps Jussieu could install himself on the landing, as soon as people have stopped coming in and out. He can tell the concierge, but ask her to keep quiet about it."

"Right, Chief."

"Call me back here in two hours, no matter what happens."

"So long as the bistro is still open."

"If not, I may come around there myself."

There was no gun in the apartment, certainly, but hadn't Léontine Faverges's murderer used a knife, which, moreover, had not been recovered? An extremely sharp knife, the experts maintained, and they thought it was probably a butcher's knife.

All the Paris cutlers, all the hardware shops had been questioned, and of course it had proved useless.

Come to think of it, nothing was known, except that a woman and a little girl were dead, that a certain navy-blue suit belonging to Gaston Meurant had spots of blood on it, and that the man's wife, at the time of the crime, was meeting a lover several times a week in a hotel on Rue Victor-Massé.

That was all. For lack of proof, the jury had just acquitted the frame-maker.

They had found it impossible to declare him guilty,

but they had found it equally impossible to declare him innocent.

While her husband was in prison, Ginette Meurant had led an exemplary life, hardly ever leaving home, never meeting anyone suspicious.

There was no telephone in their apartment. Her mail had been watched, with no result.

"Are you serious about going over there tonight?"

"Just to have a little walk before going to bed."

"Are you afraid something will happen?"

What answer could he give? That the two of them were so ill-suited, living together in the strange apartment where *The History of the Consulate and the Empire* stood on the shelves of the cozy corners next to the silk dolls and the movie stars' confessions.

Five

At about eleven-thirty, Maigret had stopped for a moment in a taxi on Boulevard de Charonne. Jussieu, wearing the blank expression of men on night duty, had appeared silently out of the shadows, had pointed above them to a lighted window on the third floor. It was one of only a few lights still on in the neighborhood, a district where people leave for work early in the morning.

Rain was still falling, but the drops were well spaced and there were the beginnings of a silver glow between the clouds.

"That window up there is the dining room," the detective, smelling strongly of cigarette smoke, had explained. "The light's been off in the bedroom for the past half hour."

Maigret waited a few minutes, hoping to catch a glimpse of life behind the curtain. Since nothing stirred, he went home to bed.

From reports and telephone calls next day, he was to reconstruct, then follow hour by hour, every movement of the Meurants.

At six o'clock in the morning, when the concierge was bringing in the trash cans, two other detectives had arrived to take over, although this time one did not go inside the house, since it was no longer possible to stay on the stairs during the daytime.

Vacher, who had spent the night there, sometimes sitting on a step, sometimes, if there was a sound of movement in the apartment, leaning against the door, made a report that was a little disturbing.

Quite early in the evening, after a meal during which the couple had hardly exchanged a word, Ginette Meurant had gone into the bedroom to get undressed; Jussieu, who had seen her, from out on the street, pulling her dress off over her head, as in a Chinese lantern show, confirmed this.

Her husband had not followed her. She had gone to him to say something, but then apparently went to bed while he remained sitting in an armchair in the dining room.

Later on, several times, he got up, walked around the room, stopping and starting repeatedly, only to sit down again.

Toward midnight his wife had gone in and spoken to him again. From the landing Vacher could not make out what they were saying, but he recognized their voices. From the tone, they were not quarreling. It was a kind of monologue from the young woman, with an occasional very brief sentence, or just a single word, from her husband.

She had gone back to bed, still by herself seemingly. The light had remained burning in the dining room, and at about half past two Ginette had returned once more.

Meurant had not been asleep, since he had replied at once, laconically. Vacher thought she had wept.

He had certainly heard a monotonous complaining, punctuated by characteristic sniffling.

Still without any sign of anger, the husband had sent her back to bed and probably dozed off at last in the armchair.

Later, a baby had woken up on the floor above; there had been muffled footsteps; then from about five o'clock the occupants of the house had started to get up, turn on the lights; the smell of coffee had spread to the staircase. At half past five, one man, already leaving for work, had looked inquisitively at the detective, who had no means of hiding, then looked at the door and seemed to understand.

It was Dupeu and Baron who took over, outside, at six o'clock. The rain had stopped. The trees were dripping. The fog reduced visibility to about twenty yards.

The light in the dining room had still been on, the one in the bedroom off. It had not been long before Meurant left the house, unshaven, his clothes crumpled, like those of a man who has spent the night fully dressed, and he had set off to the bar on the corner, where he had drunk three cups of black coffee and eaten some croissants. Just as he was turning the door handle to leave, he had changed his mind and, going back to the counter, had ordered a cognac, which he had swallowed in one gulp.

The investigations in the spring had revealed that he was not much of a drinker, that he hardly took anything except a little wine with his meals and an occasional glass of beer in the summer.

He had gone by foot to Rue de la Roquette, had not turned around to see if he was being followed.

When he arrived at his store, he had stopped outside a moment in front of the closed shutters, had not gone in, but had turned into the courtyard and unlocked the door of his glass-fronted workshop.

He had remained standing inside for quite a while, doing nothing, just staring about him at the workbench, the tools hooked on the wall, the hanging frames, the boards, and the shavings. Water had seeped in under the door and formed a little puddle on the cement floor.

Meurant had opened the stove door, put in some kindling wood, some nuts of coal that were still left. Then, as he was about to strike a match, he had changed his mind, gone outside again, and locked the door behind him.

He had walked quite a long way, with no apparent destination. At Place de la République he had gone into another bar, where he had drunk a second brandy while the waiter kept staring at him, apparently wondering where he had seen that face before.

Did he realize it? Two or three passers-by had also turned around to look at him, since his photograph was appearing in the papers that very morning under the heading GASTON MEURANT ACQUITTED.

He might have seen the headline, the photograph, on all the newsstands, but he had not been curious enough to buy himself a paper. He had taken a bus, got out twenty minutes later at Place Pigalle, and walked in the direction of Rue Victor-Massé.

Finally he had stopped in front of the small hotel kept by Nicolas Cajou, the Hotel du Lion, and had stood there a long time, staring at the façade.

When he had begun his tour again, it was to go

back down toward the Grands Boulevards, walking in a vague way, sometimes stopping at cross streets as if he were not sure where to go, buying a packet of cigarettes en route. . . .

Going along Rue Montmartre, he had reached Les Halles, and the detective had almost lost track of him in the throng. At Châtelet he had drunk a third cognac, in one gulp, as before, and he had finally arrived at Quai des Orfèvres.

Now that the sun had risen, the yellowy fog was becoming less thick. Maigret, in his office, received a telephone report from Dupeu, who had remained on guard on Boulevard de Charonne.

"The wife got up at ten to eight. I saw her open the curtains, then the window, and gaze out into the street. She looked as though she was searching for her husband. She probably didn't hear him go out and was surprised to find the dining room empty. I think she noticed me, Chief. . . ."

"Never mind. But if she goes out as well, make sure she doesn't give you the slip."

On the quay, Gaston Meurant was hesitating, looking at the windows of Police Headquarters in the same way as he had looked at those of the hotel a short while before. It was half past nine. He walked on as far as Pont Saint-Michel, was about to cross the bridge when he retraced his steps, and, going past the policeman on duty, at last came into the entrance hall.

He was familiar with the place. He was seen to climb the gray staircase slowly, stopping, not for breath, but because he was still uncertain.

"He's on his way up, Chief!" Baron telephoned, from an office on the ground floor.

And Maigret repeated to Janvier, who was with him in his office:

"He's on his way up."

They both waited. It took a long time. Meurant could not make up his mind, wandered along the corridor, stopped outside the chief inspector's door, as if he were about to knock on it without having himself announced.

"What are you looking for?" Joseph, the old porter, asked him.

"I'd like to speak to Inspector Maigret."

"Come along, then. You'll have to fill out a form."

Pencil in hand, he was pondering again whether to give up and go, just when Janvier came out of Maigret's office.

"Have you come to see the chief inspector? Follow me."

The whole thing must have been like a nightmare for Meurant. He had the face of someone who had hardly slept, his eyes red-rimmed, and he smelled of stale smoke and alcohol. Yet he was by no means drunk. He followed Janvier. The latter opened the door for him, ushered him in ahead, and then closed it again without going in himself.

Maigret, at his desk, apparently deep in the perusal of a file, waited for a while without raising his head; then he turned toward his visitor, without any sign of surprise, and murmured:

"One moment . . ."

He wrote some notes on a document, then another, murmured distractedly:

"Sit down."

Meurant did not sit down, did not even come forward into the center of the room. At the end of his patience, he announced:

"I suppose you think I've come to thank you?"

His voice was not entirely natural. He was a little hoarse and he tried to put some sarcasm into his reproach.

"Sit down," Maigret repeated, without looking at him.

This time Meurant came forward three steps, grasped the back of a chair, the seat of which was upholstered in green velvet.

"Did you do that to save me?"

The chief inspector finally surveyed him, calmly, from top to toe.

"You looked tired, Meurant."

"I'm not worried about myself, but about what you did yesterday."

His voice was more hollow, as though it was an effort for him to control his temper.

"I've come here to tell you that I don't believe a word of what you said, that you lied, like those others lied, that I'd sooner be in prison, that it was a dirty trick you played. . . ."

Was it the alcohol that made him somewhat disjointed? Possibly. Yet, again, he was not drunk, and these sentences must have been running around in his head for a good part of the night.

"Sit down."

At last! He complied against his will, as if he smelled a trap.

"You may smoke if you wish."

As a protest, so as not to be obliged to the chief inspector for anything, he did not do so, much though he wanted to, and his hand was trembling.

"It's easy for you to make people like that say what you want them to; they depend on the police. . . ."

He obviously meant Nicolas Cajou, renting rooms by the hour in his hotel, and the chambermaid.

Maigret lit his pipe slowly, waited.

"You know as well as I do that it's untrue. . . ."

His anguish brought out drops of sweat on his forehead. Maigret spoke at last.

"You mean to tell me that you murdered your aunt and little Cécile Perrin?"

"You know very well I didn't."

"I don't *know* it, but I am almost convinced that you didn't. Why, do you suppose?"

Surprised, Meurant could not think of an answer.

"There are a lot of children in the building where you live on Boulevard de Charonne, aren't there?"

Meurant said yes, mechanically.

"You hear them coming in and going out. Sometimes when they come back from school they play on the stairs. Do you talk to them sometimes?"

"I know them all right."

"You know the school hours, although you have no children yourself. That made quite an impression on me, from the beginning of the investigations. Cécile Perrin used to attend kindergarten. Léontine Faverges went to get her every day, except on Thursdays, at four o'clock in the afternoon. Until four o'clock, therefore, your aunt was alone in the apartment."

Meurant was doing his best to follow.

"You had a large bill falling due on February 28th, we know. It is possible that the last time you borrowed money from her Léontine Faverges let you know that she would not fork out again. Supposing you planned to kill her, to get your hands on the money in the Chinese vase and the bonds . . ."

"I did not kill her."

"Let me finish. Just suppose, I'm saying, that you had conceived this idea, there would have been absolutely no point in your going to Rue Manuel after four o'clock and consequently being obliged to kill two people instead of one. Criminals who murder children unnecessarily are very rare and they fall into a well-defined category."

It seemed as though Meurant, his eyes misting over, was on the point of bursting into tears.

"The murderer of Léontine Faverges and the child either was not aware of the existence of the latter or was forced to do the deed in the late afternoon. Well, if he knew the secret of the vase and the drawer with the bearer bonds in it, it is more than likely that he also knew of Cécile Perrin's presence in the apartment."

"What are you getting at?"

"Please have a cigarette."

Automatically the man obeyed, but continued to look at Maigret with suspicion in his eyes, even if the anger was now dimmed.

"We're still just supposing, aren't we? The murderer knows that you're due to arrive at Rue Manuel at about six o'clock. He is not unaware of the fact that police doctors—the newspapers have said so often enough—are capable of pinpointing the time of death in most cases to within an hour or two.''

''Nobody knew that . . .''

His voice had altered too and he was now looking away from the chief inspector's face.

''If he committed the crime at about five o'clock, the murderer could be pretty well sure that you would be suspected. He could not foresee that a customer would turn up at your workshop at six o'clock, and, anyhow, the music teacher was not able to supply any absolute evidence, since he isn't positive about the date.''

''Nobody knew . . .'' repeated Meurant mechanically.

Maigret changed the subject suddenly.

''Do you know your neighbors on Boulevard de Charonne?''

''I say good morning to them on the stairs.''

''They never call on you, even for a cup of coffee? You don't visit their apartments? You are not on more or less friendly terms with any of them?''

''No.''

''So the chances are that they have never heard your aunt mentioned.''

''They have now!''

''But not before. Did you and your wife have many friends in Paris?''

Meurant replied with bad grace, as if he were afraid that if he conceded one point he would have to give in all along the line.

''What difference does that make?''

''Did you sometimes eat out with friends?''

''No.''

"Who did you go out with on Sundays?"

"With my wife."

"And she has no relatives in Paris. Nor have you, apart from your brother, who lives mostly in the south, and with whom you broke off all contact two years ago."

"There was no quarrel."

"Nevertheless, you stopped seeing him."

And once again Maigret seemed to change the subject.

"How many keys are there to your apartment?"

"Two. My wife has one, I have the other."

"It never happens that one of you leaves the key with the concierge or a neighbor when you go out?"

Meurant preferred to keep quiet, realizing that Maigret never said anything without a reason, but unable to see what he was driving at now.

"On that day, the lock had not been forced, so the experts say who examined it. Yet, if you did not commit the murder, somebody entered your apartment twice, the first time to get your blue suit from the closet in the bedroom, and the second time to put it back, neatly enough for you to notice nothing amiss. Do you admit this?"

"I admit nothing. All I know is that my wife . . ."

"When you first met her, eight years ago, you were a lonely man. Or am I mistaken?"

"I worked all day, and in the evening I used to read. Sometimes I went to the movies."

"Did she throw herself at you?"

"No."

"Didn't other men, other customers at the restaurant where she was a waitress, make advances to her?''

He clenched his fists.

''So what?''

''How long did it take you before she finally agreed to go out with you?''

''Three weeks.''

''What did you do, that first evening?''

''We went to the movies, then she wanted to go dancing.''

''Are you a good dancer?''

''No.''

''Did she tease you about it?''

He didn't answer, more and more disconcerted by the turn the interview had taken.

''Afterward you took her back to your place?''

''No.''

''Why not?''

''Because I was in love with her.''

''And the second time?''

''We went to the movies again.''

''Afterward?''

''To a hotel.''

''Why not to your apartment?''

''Because I was living in a badly furnished room at the end of a courtyard.''

''Were you already intending to marry her and were you afraid you might put her off?''

''I wanted her to be my wife from the start.''

''Were you aware that she had many friends?''

''That's nobody's business but her own. She was free.''

''Did you talk to her about your job, your store?

You already had a store on Faubourg Saint-Antoine, unless I'm mistaken.''

"Naturally I talked to her about it.''

"Did you not have the idea at the back of your head that it might tempt her? By marrying you she would become the wife of a shopkeeper.''

Meurant was blushing.

"Do you realize now that it was you who wanted to get her and that you were prepared to cheat a little with that in view? Were you in debt?''

"No.''

"Any savings?''

"No.''

"Didn't she say anything to you about her wish to own a restaurant one day?''

"Several times.''

"What did you reply to that?''

"That it was a possibility.''

"Did you have any intention of giving up your job?''

"Not at that time.''

"You only decided to later, after about three years of marriage, when she brought up the subject again and mentioned an exceptional opportunity for it.''

He was distressed, and Maigret went on, implacably:

"You were jealous. It was your jealousy that forced her to stay at home instead of going out to work as she wanted to. You were living in a small two-room apartment then, on Rue de Turenne. Every evening you insisted that she account for her movements during the day. Were you really convinced that she loved you?''

"I thought so."

"Without any misgivings?"

"They didn't exist."

"You saw quite a lot of your brother, I believe?"

"He was living in Paris."

"Did he take your wife out?"

"We sometimes went out together, the three of us."

"They never went alone?"

"Occasionally."

"Your brother was living in a hotel, on Rue Bréa, near Place des Ternes. Did your wife ever visit his room there?"

Tormented, Meurant almost screamed:

"No!"

"Did she once own a sweater, the kind people wear skiing, a sweater made of thick white wool, hand-knitted, with reindeer designs in black and brown on it? Did she ever go out in it, in winter, wearing a pair of black slacks tight around the ankle?"

Frowning, he stared intently at Maigret.

"What are you trying to get at?"

"Answer me."

"Yes. But rarely. I didn't like her going out in the street in trousers."

"Have you often met women in the streets of Paris dressed like that?"

"No."

"Read this, Meurant."

Maigret extracted a sheet of paper from a file, the evidence of the manageress of the hotel on Rue Bréa. She distinctly remembered having had a guest named Alfred Meurant, who took a room in her place by the month for quite a long time, and sometimes came back for a few days after that. He brought lots of women to his room. Without hesitation she recognized the photograph that was shown her, the one of Ginette Meurant. She even recalled seeing her in an unusual outfit. . . .

There followed the description of the sweater and the slacks.

Had Ginette Meurant been back to Rue Bréa recently?

The proprietress's reply: Less than a year ago, when Alfred Meurant was in Paris on a brief trip.

"It's not true!" the man protested, pushing away the paper.

"Would you like me to give you the whole file to read? There are at least thirty statements, all from hotel proprietors, including one from Saint-Cloud. Did your brother once own a sky-blue convertible?"

Meurant's face provided the answer.

"He was not the only one. At the dance hall on Rue Gravilliers your wife was known to have had about fifteen lovers."

Maigret, grave and somber, was filling another pipe. It was with a heavy heart that he had given this twist to the interview.

"It's not true!" muttered the husband once more.

"She did not ask to be your wife. She did nothing to help it along. She took three weeks before she made up her mind to go out with you, perhaps because she didn't want to hurt your feelings. She went with you to the hotel when you asked her, since for her that was of little importance. You flashed before her eyes a picture of a pleasant, easy existence, security, a step up into a more or less middle-class world. You half promised her that one day you would make her dream of owning a small restaurant come true.

"Out of jealousy, you stopped her from working.

"You didn't dance. You weren't very fond of the movies."

"We used to go once a week."

"The rest of the time she was forced to go by herself. In the evenings, you used to read."

"I've always dreamed of educating myself."

"And she's always dreamed something different. Are you beginning to understand?"

"I don't believe you."

"Nevertheless, you are sure that you spoke to nobody about the Chinese vase. And on February 27th you were not wearing your blue suit. You and your wife were the only ones with keys to the apartment on Boulevard de Charonne."

The telephone rang. Maigret lifted the receiver.

"Yes, it's me. . . ."

It was Baron at the other end of the line.

"She went out about nine o'clock, four minutes to, to be precise, and she set off for Boulevard Voltaire."

"Wearing what?"

"A flowered dress and a brown woolen coat. No hat."

"What happened?"

"She went into a store that sells travel goods and bought a cheap suitcase. She came back to the apartment carrying the case. It must be warm in there, because she's opened the window. Now and then I see her walking back and forth and I presume she's packing her bags.''

While he listened, Maigret was watching Meurant, who suspected that they were talking about his wife, and looked worried.

"Has anything happened to her?" he asked at that moment.

Maigret shook his head.

"The concierge has a telephone," Baron went on, "so I sent for a taxi, which is now parked a hundred yards down the street in case she wants to call one."

"Very good. Keep in touch."

And, to Meurant:

"Just a moment . . ."

The chief inspector went into the duty room, spoke to Janvier:

"You'd better take one of the cars and go over there, to Boulevard de Charonne, as quickly as you can. It looks as if Ginette Meurant's about to take off. Perhaps she suspects her husband has come here. She must be pretty scared."

"What's his reaction?"

"I'd sooner not be in his shoes."

Maigret would sooner have had nothing to do with the whole business.

"You're wanted on the telephone, Chief Inspector."

"I'll take it."

It was the public prosecutor, whose conscience was also troubling him a little.

"Has anything happened?"

"They went home. Apparently they slept in separate rooms. Meurant went out early and at the moment he's in my office."

"What have you told him? I presume he can't hear what you're saying?"

"I'm in the duty room. He's not yet sure whether to believe me. He's struggling. He's beginning to realize that he had better face reality."

"You're not afraid he'll . . ."

"It's more than likely that he won't find her home when he gets back. She's packing her bags now."

"And what if he does find her?"

"After the treatment I've been forced to inflict on him, it's not so much her he's going to have a grudge against."

"He's not the suicidal type?"

"Not so long as he hasn't got to the bottom of it all."

"Are you planning to reveal it to him?"

Maigret said nothing, shrugged his shoulders.

"As soon as you have any news . . ."

"I'll telephone you or come around to your office, sir."

"Have you read the papers?"

"Only the headlines."

Maigret hung up. Janvier had already left. It would be wise to hold on to Meurant for a while, to prevent him catching his wife in the midst of her preparations for departure.

If he found her later on, it would be less serious. The most dangerous moment would be over. This explained why Maigret, pipe in mouth, paced up and down, strolled for a while in the long corridor, which was not so overheated.

Then, glancing at his watch, he went into his office, and found Meurant calmer, looking thoughtful.

"There is one possibility that you haven't mentioned," Ginette's husband objected. "One person, at least, must have known the secret of the Chinese vase."

"The child's mother?"

"Yes: Juliette Perrin. She often visited Léontine Faverges and Cécile. Even if the old lady had said nothing to her about her money, the child might have seen . . ."

"Do you imagine that I haven't thought of this?"

"Then why have you made no investigations there? Juliette Perrin works in a nightclub. She hangs around with all sorts of people. . . ."

He was clinging to this hope desperately, and Maigret felt unhappy about disillusioning him. Nevertheless, it was necessary.

"We've made inquiries about all her contacts, without coming up with anything.

"Besides, there is something that neither Juliette Perrin nor her casual or regular lovers could have procured without the very definite complicity of someone else."

"What?"

"The blue suit. You know the child's mother?"

"No."

"You never met her at Rue Manuel?"

"No. I knew that Cécile's mother was a nightclub entertainer, but I never had the chance to see her with my own eyes."

"Don't forget either that her daughter was killed."

For Meurant, yet another way out had been closed. He was still looking for a solution, feeling around, determined not to admit the truth.

"My wife might have mentioned it without think-ing."

"To whom?"

"I don't know."

"And given away the key to your apartment, still without thinking, before she went to the movies?"

Telephone. Janvier this time, a little out of breath.

"I'm phoning from the concierge's, Chief. The person concerned left in a taxi with the suitcase and a rather full brown handbag. I took the cab number, in case. It's from a Levallois company, and it will be easy to find it again. Baron's following her in an-other taxi. Shall I wait here?"

"Yes."

"Is he still with you?"

"Yes."

"I suppose I'd better stay put when he arrives."

"It would be wise."

"I'll park the car near one of the gates of the cemetery. It will be less noticed there. Are you plan-ning to let him go soon?"

"Yes."

Meurant was still trying to puzzle it out, and the effort required made the blood rush to his head. He was almost dropping with tiredness, with despair as well, but he succeeded in going on, and even almost in smiling.

"That's my wife they're keeping their eye on?"

Maigret nodded assent.

"I suppose they'll be keeping the same sort of eye on me?"

A vague gesture from the chief inspector.

"I haven't got a gun, I promise you!"

"I know."

"I'm not intending to kill anyone, not even myself."

"I know that too."

"Not now, at any rate."

He got to his feet, hesitating, and Maigret realized that he was reaching the point of crisis, that the man was keeping a hold on himself so that he wouldn't burst into tears, sob, bang the walls with his clenched fists.

"Try to bear up."

Meurant turned his head away, walked toward the door, attempting to keep his balance. The chief inspector placed a hand on his shoulder for a second, gently.

"Come and see me when you want to."

Meurant left the room at last without showing his face, without saying thank you, and the door shut behind him.

Baron was waiting on the quay, ready to start shadowing him again.

Six

At midday, when he was getting ready to go home for lunch, Maigret heard his first news of Ginette Meurant.

It came thrugh Dupeu, who telephoned from a bistro on Rue Delambre, in the Montparnasse area, near Rue de la Gaité. Dupeu was an excellent detective, who had only one fault: he recited his reports in a monotonous voice, as if he would never get to the end, amassing so many details that you eventually listened to him with only half an ear.

"Get on! . . . Get on with it! . . ." was what you always wanted to say to him.

If you unfortunately went so far as to do so, he would seem so miserable that you immediately regretted it.

"I'm in a place called the Pickwick, Chief, a hundred yards from Boulevard Montparnasse, and about ten minutes ago she arrived at the Hotel de Concarneau, opposite. It's a decent enough hotel, which prides itself on having hot and cold running water, a bathroom on each floor. She has room 32 and she doesn't seem likely to leave in a hurry since she argued about the prices and has taken her room on a weekly basis. Unless that's all a ruse.''

"She knows she's been followed?''

"I'm positive she does. In the taxi she looked around several times. As soon as they left Boulevard de Charonne, she showed the driver a calling card she took out of her handbag. When we reached Boulevard Saint-Michel, one behind the other, she leaned forward to the driver. I could see her clearly through the window at the back. He immediately swung right, into Faubourg Saint-Germain, then drove around, for nearly ten minutes, in the little streets of Saint-Germain-des-Prés.

"I suppose she was hoping to throw me off. When she realized that wasn't possible, she gave further directions, and before long her taxi drew up outside a building on Rue Monsieur-le-Prince.''

Maigret was listening patiently, without interrupting.

"She told the taxi to wait and went in. I went in a little after her and questioned the concierge. The person Ginette Meurant went to see is none other than Attorney Lamblin, who lives on the second floor. She stayed in the building about twenty minutes. When she came out, she didn't look very reassured and she immediately told the driver to bring her here. I suppose I'm to go on keeping a lookout?''

"Until someone comes to relieve you.''

Now, Janvier was probably still on Boulevard de Charonne, keeping an eye on the husband, together with Baron.

Had Ginette Meurant called on the lawyer merely to ask for his advice? Maigret suspected otherwise. Before leaving Police Headquarters, he gave Lucas

some instructions, then made his way toward the bus
stop.

Seven months before, on February 27th, the
Meurants had hardly any money, since they were in
no position to meet the bill of exchange that would
fall due the next day. Besides this, they had unpaid
accounts with the neighboring shops, but that, it was
true, was not unusual for them.

A few days later, when the examining magistrate
had asked Meurant to name a lawyer, the frame-
maker had objected that he did not have the means to
pay for one, and Pierre Duché had been appointed by
the court.

What had Ginette Meurant been living on in the
meantime? As far as the police knew—and they had
watched her incoming mail—she had received no
money orders. Nor, apparently, had she cashed any
checks. Although she had incurred very few expenses
and had led a quiet existence in her apartment, she
had still had to eat, and, before the trial, she had
bought the skirt and black coat that she wore to
court.

Perhaps the answer was that she had been putting
money aside herself, without her husband knowing,
cheating him of some of the housekeeping money, as
quite a few wives do?

Lamblin, at the Law Courts, had got hold of her.
The lawyer was smart enough to recognize that the
case would have spectacular repercussions, and to
know that it would bring him a great deal of publicity
if he then represented the young woman.

Maigret might be making a mistake, but he was
convinced that Ginette Meurant had gone to Rue

Monsieur-le-Prince to get hold of some money, rather than to ask for advice.

Lamblin's reputation being what it was, he must have given her some money, but only in dribs and drabs. He had probably also advised her not to leave Paris, but to stay calmly where she was and wait for new developments.

The Montparnasse neighborhood had not been chosen by chance. Neither Meurant nor Ginette had lived around there or was known there, and it was most unlikely that Meurant would look for his wife in that area.

The chief inspector returned to the peaceful atmosphere of his apartment, had lunch alone with Madame Maigret, and when he arrived back at the Quai, at two o'clock, he had a telephone call from Janvier to say that Meurant had not left the apartment, where everything was quiet.

He had to go a meeting with the director to discuss a disagreeable case, which had political implications, and it was four o'clock before Janvier called again.

"Things are moving, Chief. I can't say what's going to happen, but there will be a development soon, I'm sure. He left home at two-forty-five, carrying a number of large parcels. Although they seemed heavy, he didn't call a taxi. Still, he didn't have far to go. After a short distance he went into a second-hand shop, on Boulevard de Ménilmontant, and stayed there some time talking to the owner."

"Did he see you?"

"Probably. It was hard to keep out of sight, since the neighborhood was pretty deserted. He sold his watch, the phonograph, some records, a pile of books.

Then he went back home, came out again, this time with an enormous bundle wrapped up in a sheet.

"He returned to the same shop, where he sold some clothes, linen, blankets, and some brass candlesticks.

"He's at home now. I don't think it'll be for long."

In fact, Janvier called back in fifty minutes' time.

"He left the apartment once again and went to Faubourg Saint-Antoine, to another frame-maker's. They had quite a long conversation, then the man took Meurant in his truck to Rue de la Roquette, where they stopped opposite the shop you know.

"They inspected the frames one by one. The man from Fabourg Saint-Antoine loaded a number of them into his truck and handed over some money to Meurant.

"I forgot to tell you that he's shaved now. I don't know what he's up to in his workshop, but the car's only a few yards away, just in case. . . ."

At six o'clock Maigret received his last telephone call from Janvier, who was calling from Gare de Lyon.

"He's due to leave in about fifteen minutes, Chief. He bought a second-class ticket for Toulon. He only has one small bag with him. At the moment, he's drinking a brandy in the bar; I can see him through the window of the phone booth."

"Is he watching you?"

"Yes."

"How does he seem?"

"Like a man who's got no time for anything else but the one idea he's got fixed in his mind."

"Make sure he really gets on that train and come back here."

The train stopped only at Dijon, Lyons, Avignon, and Marseilles. Maigret made calls to the police at each of the stations, gave them the frame-maker's description and the number of the car he was in. Then he called the Flying Squad at Toulon.

The chief inspector in charge there was named Blanc and he was about the same age as Maigret. They knew each other well, because, before entering the national crime force, Blanc had been at the Quai des Orfèvres.

"It's Maigret. Look, old man, I hope you're not too busy. I'm arranging for the public prosecutor's department to send you a judicial warrant tomorrow, but I thought I'd better put you in the picture as soon as possible. What time does the six-seventeen from Paris arrive at Toulon?"

"Eight-thirty-two."

"Good. In car number 10—that's assuming that he hasn't changed his seat during the trip—you will find a man by the name of Meurant."

"I've been reading the papers."

"I'd like him to be shadowed as soon as he steps off the train.

"That's easy. Does he know the town?"

"I don't think he's ever been to the South before, but I may be mistaken. Meurant has a brother named Alfred."

"I know the one. I've had quite a lot of trouble with him."

"Is he in Toulon at the moment?"

"I can let you know in an hour or two. Shall I call you back?"

"Yes, please, at my home."

He gave his number on Boulevard Richard-Lenoir.

"What do you know about Alfred Meurant's activities lately?"

"He normally lives in a boardinghouse called 'The Eucalyptus,' outside town, quite a way out, on the hill between the Faron and La Vallette."

"What kind of place is it?"

"The kind we keep an eye on. There are quite a few like it along the coast between Marseilles and Menton. The owner is a man named Lisca, known as Freddo, who was for a long time a bartender in Montmartre, on Rue de Douai. Freddo married a pretty kid, a former striptease dancer, and they bought The Eucalyptus.

"Freddo does the cooking, and they say he's marvelous at it too. The house is off the main road, at the end of a lane that leads nowhere. In summer they eat outside under the trees.

"Quite respectable people from Toulon—doctors, civil servants, magistrates—go there for a meal from time to time.

"But the bulk of the customers are the crooks who live along the coast and periodically go up to Paris.

"A few tarts too, who come down for a rest cure.

"Get the setting?"

"I get it."

"Two frequent customers, almost all-year-round boarders, are Falconi and Scapucci."

Two men with a string of convictions behind them, who cropped up periodically around Pigalle.

"They are great friends of Alfred Meurant's. The three of them go around openly, putting slot machines in local bars. They also provide them with none-too-virtuous barmaids, whom they collect from all over the place.

"They have several cars at their disposal and change them pretty frequently. For some time now I've been suspecting them of selling cars in Italy that have been stolen and repainted in Paris and the suburbs.

"I've got no proof yet. My men are on it."

"I have good reason to think that Gaston Meurant will try to contact his brother."

"If he asks at the right places, he won't have much trouble finding him, unless his brother's covering his tracks."

"If my Meurant should buy a gun or try to get hold of one, I would like to be informed immediately."

"Right, Maigret. We'll do our best. What's the weather like up there?

"Gray and cold."

"Sun's shining nicely here. By the way, I almost forgot someone. Among Freddo's customers at the moment is a fellow named Kubik."

Twelve years before, Maigret had arrested him after a jewel robbery on Boulevard Saint-Martin.

"It's more than likely he was involved in the jewel theft last month on Cours Albert-Premier in Nice."

Maigret was familiar with the underworld down there also, and he envied Blanc a little. Like most of his colleagues, he preferred to deal with professionals, since one knew at once with them the kind of ground on which the match would be played and there were definite rules for the game.

How was Gaston Meurant, alone in a corner of his compartment, going to cope with people like that?

Maigret spent some time with Lucas, whom he put in charge of organizing the watch being kept on Rue Delambre and appointing detectives to go there in shifts.

Ginette Meurant had spent the afternoon in her hotel bedroom, more than likely asleep. As the notice stated on the outside of the building, there was a telephone in each room, but all calls had to go through the switchboard.

According to the proprietor, who came from the Auvergne, she had not used the telephone, and he was positive that nobody at the hotel had put a call through to the South. Nonetheless, there was a special operator tapping the line.

Ginette had stuck it out for a long time. Either she had been extraordinarily cunning, since the murder on Rue Manuel, or she had not once tried to communicate with the man who had been accompanying her to Rue Victor-Massé for several months, up to and including February 26th.

It was almost as if this man, suddenly, from one day to the next, had ceased to exist. Nor did he, for his part, seem to have made any attempt to get in touch with her.

The police had considered the possibility of prearranged signals. They had kept a close watch on the windows on Boulevard de Charonne, studied the position of the curtains, which might have carried some significance, the lights in the apartment, the movements of people on the opposite sidewalk.

Nor had the man put in any appearance in the courtroom or in the neighborhood of the Law Courts.

It was so remarkable that Maigret was very impressed.

Now, she was going out at last, looking for a cheap restaurant in this district new to her, eating alone at a table, reading a magazine. Then she was off to buy some more at the corner of Boulevard Montparnasse, plus a few romantic novels, was climbing back up to her room, where the light remained on until past midnight.

Gaston Meurant was still in the moving train. At Dijon, then at Lyons, a detective walked along the corridors, ascertained that he was still in his corner, and the information was telephoned to Boulevard Richard-Lenoir, where Maigret stretched his arm out in the dark to pick up the receiver.

Another day was beginning. Past Montélimar, Meurant was discovering the atmosphere of Provence, and probably his nose was soon pressed against the window as he watched a strange landscape pass by in the sunshine.

Marseilles . . . Maigret was shaving when he had the call from Gare Saint-Charles.

Meurant was still on the train, which was now on its way again. He had not tricked them. He really was going to Toulon.

In Paris the weather remained gray, and, in the bus, people's faces were downcast or sullen. On his desk, a pile of administrative mail awaited him.

A detective—Maigret had lost track of who it was—telephoned from the bistro on Rue Delambre.

"She's asleep. The curtains are closed, at any rate, and she hasn't ordered any breakfast."

The train arrived at Toulon. Gaston Meurant, bag in hand, a policeman on his heels, wandered around the main square disoriented, and eventually walked into the Hotel des Voyageurs, where he chose the cheapest room.

A little later, the police were convinced that he did not know the town, because he began to lose himself in the streets. After some trouble, he reached Boulevard de Strasbourg, where he went into a large café. He ordered coffee this time, not brandy, asked several questions of the waiter, who did not seem able to furnish the required information.

At noon he had not found what he was after, and, comically, it was Chief Inspector Blanc who was getting impatient.

"I wanted to have a glimpse of your fellow myself," he said to Maigret on the telephone. "I found him in a bar on Quai Cronstadt. He could not have slept much on the train. He looked like some poor fellow absolutely knocked out by lack of sleep but obsessed by some crazy idea. He's not going about it the right way. Up till now he's been in about fifteen cafés and bars. Each time, he orders mineral water. He appears so much to be a man begging for something that everyone looks at him sideways. He always asks the same question:

" 'Do you know Alfred Meurant?'

"Bartenders and waiters are immediately suspicious, especially the ones who do know him. Some just make a vague gesture in reply. Others ask:

" 'What's he do?'

" 'I don't know. He lives in Toulon.'

"My detective who's trailing him is beginning to feel sorry for him and almost wants to help him out.

"At the rate Meurant's going, this may last for ages, and he'll make himself sick on mineral water."

Maigret was familiar enough with Toulon to know of at least three places where Meurant could have found some news of his brother. The frame-maker was now, however, reaching the right end of town at last. If he went farther on into the back streets that flank Quai Cronstadt, or if chance brought him to Le Mourillon, he would doubtless eventually pick up the information he was hunting for so stubbornly.

On Rue Delambre, Ginette Meurant had opened her curtains, ordered coffee and croissants, and had gone back to bed to read.

She telephoned neither Lamblin nor anyone else. Nor did she make any attempt to find out what was happening to her husband, or if the police were still on her own tracks.

Wouldn't she collapse under the strain sooner or later?

As for the lawyer, he took no steps, but went on with his usual activities.

Maigret had an idea, went into the duty room, and walked up to Lucas.

"What time did she go and see her lawyer yesterday?"

"About eleven o'clock, if I remember rightly. I can look up my report."

"No need. In any case, she still had time to put an advertisement in the evening papers. Get hold of all yesterday's papers, this morning's as well, and, later

on, the evening editions. Go through the personal
ads.''

Lamblin did not have the reputation of being a
very scrupulous man. If Ginette Meurant asked him
to insert an advertisement, would he hesitate? It was
unlikely.

If Maigret's hunch was a good one, it would mean
that she did not know the present address of her
former lover.

On the other hand, if she knew it, and if he had
not moved since March, wouldn't Lamblin have telephoned him for her? Might she not have done it
herself, during the twenty minutes she spent in the
lawyer's office?

One detail had struck the chief inspector ever since
spring, when the case had begun. The liaison between the young woman and the man described by
Nicolas Cajou had lasted for many months. Throughout the winter they had met several times a week,
which seemed to indicate that her lover lived in
Paris.

Yet, nonetheless, they always met in a small hotel.

Didn't it seem likely that, for one reason or another, the man was unable to receive his mistress at
his home?

Was he married? Perhaps he did not live alone?

Maigret had not found the right answer.

''It's a long shot,'' he said to Lucas, ''but try to
find out if a telephone call was made to Toulon
yesterday from Lamblin's building.''

There was nothing else for him to do now but
wait. In Toulon, Gaston Meurant was still searching,
and it was not until half past four, in a little café

outside which men were playing bowls, that he at last got the information he was after.

The waiter pointed out the hill to him, launched into complicated directions.

Maigret already knew, by that time, that the brother, Alfred, was indeed in Toulon and had not left The Eucalyptus for over a week.

He gave Chief Inspector Blanc his instructions.

"Have you got among your detectives someone who wouldn't be recognized by those people?"

"My men never remain unknown for long, but I have one who arrived only three days ago. He comes from Brest, since his main job is to look after the naval docks. They've certainly not caught on to him yet."

"Send him out to The Eucalyptus."

"Right. He'll be there before Meurant; the poor fellow is either trying to save money or he has no idea of the distance, because he's set out on foot. Since he'll probably get lost two or three times on those lanes up the hill . . ."

It was agony for Maigret not to be on the spot. In spite of frequent and precise reports, he still got only secondhand information.

Two or three times during the day, he was tempted to go to Rue Delambre and renew contact with Ginette Meurant. He had the feeling—for no special reason— that he was beginning to get to know her better. Perhaps, now, he would find the right questions, the ones she might finally answer.

It was still too early. Since Meurant had gone off to Toulon like that, without hesitating, he must have had his reasons.

During the investigations, the police had got nothing out of the brother, but that did not mean that there was nothing to be got from him.

Gaston Meurant was unarmed; this was already an established fact, and, for the rest, they would have to wait.

He went home, grumpy. Madame Maigret was careful not to question him, and he had dinner in his slippers, plunged in the papers, then switched on the radio, hunted for a less talkative station, and when he failed to find one, turned it off with a comfortable sigh.

At ten o'clock at night, they called from Toulon. It wasn't Blanc, who was attending a banquet, but the young detective from Brest, named Le Goënec, whom the chief inspector of the Flying Squad had sent out to The Eucalyptus.

"I'm telephoning from the station."

"Where is Gaston Meurant?"

"In the waiting room. He's taking the night train in an hour and a half. He's paid for his hotel room."

"Did he go to The Eucalyptus?"

"Yes."

"He saw his brother?"

"Yes. When he arrived, at about six o'clock, three men were playing cards with the owner's wife in the bar. They were Kubik, Falconi, and Alfred Meurant, all three of them rather cheerful. I had arrived before him and asked if I could eat and stay for the night. The owner came out of the kitchen to inspect me and finally said I could. I was wearing a backpack and told them I was hitchhiking through the Riviera looking for work."

"Did they believe you?"

"I don't know. While waiting for dinnertime, I sat down in a corner, ordered some white wine, and started reading. They looked over at me from time to time, but they didn't seem to worry about me much. Gaston Meurant arrived a quarter of an hour after me. It was already dark. I saw the glass door open from the garden, and he remained standing on the threshold, looking around him like an owl."

"How did his brother take it?"

"He stared hard at the newcomer, stood up, threw his cards on the table, and went over to him.

" 'What do you think you're doing here? Who tipped you off I was here?'

"The others pretended not to be listening.

" 'I must speak to you, Alfred,' said Gaston Meurant.

"He added quickly:

" 'Don't be afraid. I'm not after you.'

" 'Come on!' ordered his brother, and went off toward the stairs leading to the bedrooms.

"I couldn't follow them right away. The others had stopped talking and seemed worried; they began to look at me differently. They were probably starting to connect my arrival with Meurant's.

"Anyway I went on drinking my wine and reading.

"The little house, although recently repainted, is quite old, badly built, and every sound is audible.

"The two brothers shut themselves in a bedroom on the second floor, and Alfred Meurant's voice was harsh and loud at first. You couldn't make out the words, but it was obvious he was very angry.

"Then the other, the one from Paris, began to

speak, in a much softer voice. This lasted some time, almost without interruption, as if he was telling some prepared story.

"After winking at the men, the landlady came and set my table, as if she was trying to create a diversion. Then the others ordered apéritifs. Kubik went out to look for Freddo in the kitchen, and I didn't see him again.

"I imagine that, becoming prudent, he cleared out, because I heard a car engine starting up."

"You've no idea what went on upstairs?"

"Only that they remained shut up there for an hour and a half. In the end, it seemed that it was Gaston Meurant, the one from Paris, who had the upper hand, while his brother spoke in a low voice.

"I had finished eating when they came downstairs. Alfred Meurent looked rather black, as if things hadn't worked out the way he planned, while the other fellow, on the contrary, seemed more relaxed than he had when he arrived.

" 'You'll have a drink, then?' Alfred proposed.

" 'No. Thanks all the same.'

" 'You're going right back?'

" 'Yes.'

"Then they both looked across at me, frowning.

" 'I'll drive you downtown in the car.'

" 'No, don't bother.'

" 'Do you want me to call for a taxi?'

" 'No, thanks.'

"They were both talking in undertones, and it was obvious that they were only speaking to fill an awkward gap.

"Gaston Meurant went out. His brother shut the

door, was about to say something to the landlady and Falconi when he caught sight of me and changed his mind.

"I wasn't sure what I should do then. I didn't dare telephone the chief and ask for further instructions. I thought the best thing to do was to follow Gaston Meurant. I went outside as if I were just going to get some fresh air after dinner, leaving my backpack behind.

"I caught up with my man, who was walking steadily down the road to town.

"He stopped to have a bite to eat on Boulevard de la République. Then he went to the station and found out the times of the trains. Last of all, he went to the Hotel des Voyageurs, picked up his bag, and paid his bill.

"Since then he's been waiting. He's not reading the newspapers; he's doing nothing except staring in front of him, his eyes half closed. You can't say he looks happy, but he doesn't exactly look displeased with himself."

"Wait till he gets on the train and call me back with the number of the car."

"Okay. Tomorrow morning, I'll give the chief inspector my report."

Inspector Le Goënec was about to hang up when Maigret thought of something.

"I'd like someone to make sure that Alfred Meurant does not leave The Eucalyptus."

"Do you want me to go back there? You don't think they've caught on to me?"

"All I want is for one of you to keep an eye on the house. I'd like the telephone tapped too. If they call

Paris, or any long-distance number, let me know as quickly as possible.''

The routine was starting to repeat itself, but in reverse order this time: Marseilles, Avignon, Lyons, Dijon were all alerted. Gaston Meurant was allowed to travel alone, like a grownup, but, in a way, he was being passed hand to hand.

He wouldn't be arriving in Paris until half past eleven the next morning.

Maigret went to bed. He felt as though he had just dozed off when his wife woke him with his first cup of coffee. The sky was clear at last and there was sunshine on the rooftops opposite. The people in the street were walking with a springier step.

''Will you be home for lunch?''

''I doubt it. I'll give you a call before noon.''

Ginette Meurant hadn't left Rue Delambre. She was still spending the greater part of her time in bed, going down only to eat and to stock up on magazines and novels.

''Nothing new, Maigret?'' asked the public prosecutor anxiously.

''Nothing definite yet, but I wouldn't be surprised if there was a development very shortly.''

''What's Meurant up to?''

''He's on the train.''

''Which train?''

''The one from Toulon. He's on his way back. He's been to see his brother.''

''What went on between them?''

''They had a long conversation, a bit violent at first, apparently, but then calmer. The brother is unhappy about it. Gaston Meurant, on the other hand, appears to know where he is going at last.''

What else could Maigret have said? He had no definite information to give the public prosecutor's office. For two days he had been groping his way around in a sort of fog, but, like Gaston Meurant, he nonetheless felt that things were coming to a head.

He was tempted to go to the station soon and meet the frame-maker himself. Wasn't it better that he remain at the center of operations? But if he started following Gaston Meurant through the streets, wasn't there a risk he might spoil everything?

He chose Lapointe, knowing he would be pleased, then another detective, Neveu, who had not had anything to do with the case so far. For ten years Neveu had worked on the streets of Paris and he specialized in pickpockets.

Lapointe left for the station unaware that Neveu would soon be following him.

Maigret had to give him some precise instructions beforehand.

Seven

For years Gaston Meurant, with his fresh complexion, his red hair, his blue eyes, and his sheeplike
expression, had been a timid man maybe, but above
all a patient, determined man, who had striven, in the
midst of the three million denizens of Paris, to con-
struct some small measure of happiness.

He had mastered his craft to the best of his ability,
a delicate craft that required taste and precision. One
could readily imagine how, the day he had opened
his own business, even though only at the end of a
courtyard, he had felt satisfaction from having over-
come the most difficult obstacle.

Had it been his timidity, or his cautiousness, the
fear of making a mistake, that had made him long
keep his distance from women? During the course of
the interrogations, he had admitted to Maigret that,
until meeting Ginette, he had managed with little,
with the very minimum, with furtive contacts of
which he found himself ashamed, apart from an affair he had had when he was about eighteen with a
woman much older than he, which had lasted only a
few weeks.

When the day came on which, blushing, he had at

last asked a woman to marry him, he was well over thirty, and as luck would have it, she was a girl who, a few months later, when he was impatiently expecting news of a forthcoming birth, admitted to him that she could not have a baby.

He had not rebelled. He had accepted it, as he accepted the fact that she was unlike the companion he had dreamed of.

In spite of everything, they were a married couple. He was no longer alone, even if there wasn't always a light in the window when he came home in the evening, even if it was often he who had to get the dinner ready, and even if, afterward, they had nothing to say to each other.

Her dream, on the other hand, had been of a life spent in the midst of all the activity of a restaurant she owned, and he had let her have her way, without any illusions, knowing perfectly well that the experiment could only come to grief.

Then, without a sign of bitterness, he had returned to his workshop and his picture frames, compelled, every so often, to go and ask his aunt for her help.

During those years of married life, as in the years that had preceded them, there had been no trace of anger, no trace of impatience.

He would go his own way with gentle determination, bowing his big red head when he had to, holding it high again the moment fate seemed to look more kindly on him.

All told, he had built up a little world of his own around his love, and he was doing everything in his power to cling to it.

Did not all this explain the hatred that had sud-

denly hardened his eyes when Maigret had given his
evidence in court, replacing the image he had formed
for himself of Ginette with another one?

Acquitted against his will, as it were, freed on
account of the suspicions that would thenceforth hang
over his companion, he had nonetheless left the Law
Courts with her, at her side; without linking arms,
they had returned to their apartment on Boulevard de
Charonne.

They had not slept in their bed together, however.
Twice, three times, she had gone to speak to him,
perhaps doing her utmost to tempt him, but she had
gone to sleep alone in the end, while he spent most
of the night awake in the dining room.

At that time, he was still struggling, trying not to
believe it. Perhaps he might have been able to re-
cover confidence. But would it have lasted long?
Would life have been able to start all over again as
before? Wouldn't he have undergone a series of painful makeshifts, before the ultimate crisis?

He had gone by himself, without shaving, to look
at the front of a hotel. To lend himself courage, he
had drunk three brandies. He had hesitated once
more before entering the chilly hall of the Quai des
Orfèvres.

Had Maigret been wrong to speak to him in that
brutal way, setting up the reaction that would have
been set up anyway sooner or later?

Even had he wanted to, the chief inspector could
not have acted otherwise. With Meurant acquitted,
Meurant not guilty, there was, somewhere, at liberty,
a man who had cut the throat of Léontine Faverges
and then suffocated a little girl aged four, a murderer

with enough cold blood and cunning to send another
man to trial in his place, who had been on the verge
of succeeding in his plan.

Maigret had struck while the iron was hot, forcing
Meurant in one shock to open his eyes, to look truth
in the face at last, and it had been a new man who
had left his office, a man for whom nothing mattered
any longer from now on but one fixed idea.

He had gone straight ahead, feeling neither hunger
nor fatigue, moving from one train to another, in-
capable of stopping until he reached his objective.

Did he have any inkling that the chief inspector
had established a whole network of surveillance around
him, that he had been expected at every railway
station he stopped at, and that there was continually
someone on his heels, possibly to intervene at the last
moment?

He did not seem to be concerned about it, convinced that all the wiles of the police could not
prevail against his will.

Telephone call after telephone call came in, report
after report. Lucas had minutely examined the personal advertisements in vain. The telephone tap, waiting for any calls Ginette Meurant might eventually
make from the room on Rue Delambre, had nothing
to report.

There had been no call from the lawyer Lamblin to
the South, or to any local number.

At Toulon, Alfred Meurant, the brother, had not
left The Eucalyptus, and had not telephoned anybody
either.

They faced a blank, a void in the midst of which
there was just one silent man, moving as if in a dream.

At eleven-forty, Lapointe telephoned from Gare de Lyon.

"He's just got in, Chief. He's now eating some sandwiches in the buffet. He's still got his suitcase with him. Was it you who sent Neveu to the station?"

"Yes. Why?"

"I wondered whether you wanted him to take over. Neveu's in the buffet too, quite close to Meurant."

"Don't worry about him. You carry on."

A quarter of an hour later, it was Inspector Neveu's turn to give his account.

"I did it, Chief. I jostled him at the exit. He didn't notice anything. He's got a gun. A big revolver, probably a Smith and Wesson, in the right-hand pocket of his jacket. It doesn't show too much, thanks to his raincoat."

"Has he left the station?"

"Yes. He caught a bus, and I saw Lapointe get on behind him."

"You can come back now."

Meurant had not called at any gunsmith's. It must necessarily have been at Toulon that he had obtained the revolver, which could therefore have been supplied to him only by his brother.

What exactly had occurred between the two men, upstairs in the curious family boardinghouse that was used as a crooks' meeting place?

Gaston Meurant knew now that his brother, too, had had an intimate relationship with Ginette, and yet he had not gone in order to settle accounts with him on that score.

Hadn't he hoped, in visiting Toulon, to get information about the short, very dark-haired man who, several times a week, used to take his wife to Rue Victor-Massé?

Had he some reason to think that his brother would know about it? And had he eventually got what he wanted, a name, a clue, which the police, for their part, had been searching for in vain for several months past?

It was possible. It was probable, since he had compelled his brother to hand over a gun to him.

If Alfred Meurant had talked, in any case, it couldn't have been out of brotherly affection. Had he been scared? Had Gaston threatened him? With some disclosure or other? Or with doing him in one fine day?

Maigret asked for Toulon on the phone and succeeded, after some trouble, in getting Chief Inspector Blanc on the other end.

"It's me again. I'm sorry for all the trouble I'm giving you. We may need Alfred Meurant any time now. We can't be sure of finding him when the time comes, since I wouldn't be surprised if he took it into his head to go off on a trip somewhere. At present, I have nothing to pin on him. Couldn't you have him hauled in on some more or less plausible excuse and keep him for a few hours?"

"Right. That's not difficult. I've always got a question or two I can ask any of his bunch."

"Thanks. See if you can find out if he had a pretty powerful revolver and whether it's still in his room."

"Okay. Any news?"

"Not yet."

Maigret almost added that it wouldn't be long. He had just warned his wife that he wouldn't be home to lunch, and, feeling disinclined to leave his office, he had ordered some sandwiches from the Brasserie Dauphine.

He still felt sorry not to be outside, following Gaston Meurant in person. He was smoking pipe after pipe, impatient, ceaselessly watching the telephone. The sun was shining brightly, and the yellowing leaves of the trees lent an air of gaiety to the Seine quaysides.

"That you, Chief? I have to be quick. I'm at Gare de l'Est. He's checked his bag at the luggage office and he's just bought a ticket to Chelles."

"In Seine-et-Marne?"

"Yes. The train is due to leave in a few minutes. I'd better get cracking. I'm supposed to go on following him, right?"

"What do you think!"

"No special instructions?"

What was at the back of Lapointe's mind? Had he guessed the reason for Neveu's presence at Gare de Lyon?

The chief inspector grunted:

"Nothing particular. Do what you think best."

He knew Chelles, over a dozen miles outside Paris, on the banks of the canal and the Marne. He remembered there was a big caustic-soda plant, in front of which you could always see loaded barges. Once when he had gone through the neighborhood on a Sunday morning, he had noticed a whole flotilla of canoes.

The temperature had changed in the past twenty-four hours, but whoever was in charge of the central heating in the offices of Police Headquarters had not regulated the boiler accordingly. The air was stifling.

Maigret was eating a sandwich, standing in front of the window, gazing vaguely at the Seine. From time to time he took a swig of beer, cast a questioning glance at the telephone.

The train, which stopped at all stations, would be bound to take half an hour at least, perhaps an hour, to reach Chelles.

It was the detective on duty on Rue Delambre who called first.

"Same as before, Chief. She's just gone out and is having her lunch in the same restaurant, at the same table, as if she already had her set habits."

As far as one could tell, she still had the courage not to get in touch with her lover.

Had he given her, as long ago as February, even before the double murder on Rue Manuel, her instructions for the future? Was she afraid of him?

Of the two of them, which was it who had had the idea of the telephone call that brought about the incrimination of Gaston Meurant?

For, at the beginning, he had not been suspected. He had presented himself of his own accord to the police and introduced himself as the nephew of Léontine Faverges, whose death he had just read about in the paper.

They had had no grounds for searching his home.

But someone grew impatient. Someone had been in a hurry to see the investigation take a definite direction.

Six days, seven days had passed before the anonymous telephone call that revealed what would be found in a closet on Boulevard de Charonne, a certain blue suit with bloodstains on it.

Lapointe still gave no sign of life. It was Toulon that called.

"He's in my duty room. We're asking him a few minor questions and we'll keep him until you give us further notice. We'll find some pretext, all right. His room's been searched thoroughly, without a gun being found in it. Even so, my men maintain that he often carried a revolver, which has led him to be convicted twice."

"Has he had other convictions?"

"Never anything serious, apart from proceedings for procuring. He's too clever."

"Thanks very much. Good-bye for now. I must hang up, because I'm expecting an important call any moment now."

He went into the office next door, where Janvier had just arrived.

"You'd better stay on hand, ready to leave. And make sure there's a car free in the yard."

He was beginning to regret that he had not told Lapointe everything he knew. He remembered a movie about Malaya. It had shown a native who had suddenly run amok—that is, he had been seized in a matter of seconds by a kind of sacred madness, and, walking straight ahead, his pupils dilated, a kris in his hand, he had killed every living thing in his path.

Gaston Meurant was not a Malay, nor had he run amok. Nevertheless, for more than twenty-four hours now, had he not been pursuing a fixed idea and was he not capable of disposing of anyone who might happen to stand in his way?

At last, the telephone. Maigret leaped over to it.

"Is that you, Lapointe?"

"Yes, Chief."

"At Chelles?"

"Beyond it. I don't know exactly where I am. Between the canal and the Marne, about a mile and a half from Chelles. I can't be certain, since we took a complicated route."

"Did Meurant seem to know the way?"

"He didn't ask anybody anything. He must have been given precise directions. He stopped now and then to look at signs and eventually he took a lane leading to the edge of the river. Where this lane joins the former towpath, which is now only a track, there's an inn, which is where I'm telephoning you from. The innkeeper's wife has warned me that in winter she doesn't serve meals or rent rooms. Her husband's the ferryman. Meurant went past the front of the inn without stopping.

"Two hundred yards upstream you can just see a tumble-down cottage. Geese and ducks are waddling around it."

"Is that where Meurant has gone?"

"He hasn't gone in. He spoke to an old woman, who pointed to the river."

"Where is he at the moment?"

"Standing at the edge of the water, leaning against a tree. The old woman's over eighty. She's known as Mother Goose. The innkeeper's wife maintains she's half mad. Her name is Joséphine Millard. Her husband's been dead a long time. Ever since, she's always worn the same black dress, and it's rumored locally that she doesn't take it off to go to bed. When she needs anything, she goes to the market on Saturday to sell a goose or a duck."

"Did she have any children?"

"That takes us back so long ago that the innkeeper's wife can't remember. She says it was before her time."

"Is that all?"

"No. There's a man living with her."

"Permanently?"

"For the past few months, yes. Before that, he used to disappear for several days at a time."

"What does he do?"

"Nothing. He chops wood. He reads. He fishes. He's patched up an old canoe. Just now, he's doing some fishing. I've seen him, from a distance, in the boat, which is moored to some stakes at the bend in the Marne."

"What sort of a man is he?"

"I couldn't make out. According to the innkeeper's wife, he's dark, thick-set, with a hairy chest."

"Short?"

"Yes."

There was a silence. Then, hesitantly, as if embarrassed, Lapointe asked:

"Are you coming, Chief?"

Lapointe was not afraid. Was he not feeling, however, that he would have to take responsibilities beyond his powers?

"By car, it would take you less than half an hour."

"I'll be along."

"What should I do, while I wait?"

Maigret hesitated and eventually decided to say:

"Nothing."

"Shall I stay in the inn?"

"Can you see Meurant from where you are?"

"Yes."

"In that case, stay there."

He went into the office next door, made a sign to Janvier, who was waiting. Just as he was going out, he changed his mind, went across to Lucas.

"Go up to Records and see if there's anything under the name of Millard."

"Okay, Chief. Shall I telephone you somewhere?"

"No. I don't know exactly where I'm going. The far side of Chelles, somewhere on the banks of the Marne. If you have some urgent news for me, ask at the local police station for the name of an inn about a mile and a half upstream."

Janvier took the wheel of the small black car, since Maigret had never been inclined to learn to drive.

"Anything new, Chief?"

"Yes."

The inspector did not like to press him, and after a long silence the chief inspector muttered gloomily:

"But I don't know what exactly."

He wasn't sure that he was in such a hurry to get there. He would rather not admit it, not even to himself.

"Do you know the way?"

"I once went there for lunch on a Sunday with the wife and kids."

They drove through the suburbs, past the first vacant lots, then the first fields. At Chelles they pulled up hesitantly at a crossroads.

"If it's upstream, we should turn right."

"Let's try it."

Just as they were leaving the town, a police car,

with its siren blaring, overtook them, and Janvier looked at Maigret without speaking.

The chief inspector did not say anything either. Much farther on, he said, chewing the stem of his pipe:

"I suppose it's all over."

For the police car had turned off toward the Marne, which they could now glimpse between the trees. To the right was an inn, built of yellow-painted brick. A woman, who seemed highly excited, was standing on the doorstep.

The police car, unable to get any farther, had parked by the side of the lane. Maigret and Janvier emerged from theirs. The woman, gesticulating, was calling out something to them which they couldn't catch.

They walked toward the cottage surrounded by geese and ducks. The local police, who had reached it before them, were questioning two men, who seemed to have been waiting for them. One of them was Lapointe. The other, from a distance, looked like Gaston Meurant.

There were three local policemen, including one officer. An old woman on the doorstep was looking at all these people, nodding her head, without seeming to understand exactly what was going on. Nobody, anyway, really understood, except perhaps Meurant and Lapointe.

Automatically, Maigret glanced around to look for a body, but could see none. Lapointe said to him:

"In the water . . ."

But there was nothing to be seen in the water either.

As for Gaston Meurant, he was calm, almost smiling, and when the chief inspector finally decided to look him in the face, it was as if the picture-framer were silently thanking him.

Lapointe was explaining, both for the benefit of his chief and for that of the local police:

"The man stopped fishing and shoved his boat off from the stakes you can see over there."

"Who is he?"

"I don't know his name. He was wearing denim pants and a turtleneck seaman's sweater. He began to row across the river against the current."

"Where were you?" the local police officer asked.

"At the inn. I was watching the scene from the window. I had just been on the phone to Chief Inspector Maigret . . ."

He gestured to his chief, and the officer, confused, stepped toward him.

"I beg your pardon, Chief Inspector. I never expected to see you here. That's why I didn't recognize you. Your inspector got the innkeeper's wife to telephone us, and all she said was that a man had just been killed and had fallen in the water. I immediately alerted the Flying Squad. . . ."

They heard the sound of a car engine on the other side of the inn.

"There they are!"

The newcomers added to the chaos and bewilderment. They were now in the department of Seine-et-Marne, and Maigret had no official standing in the case.

Nevertheless, everybody turned toward the chief inspector.

"Shall we handcuff him?"

"That's up to you, Lieutenant. If I were in your place, I wouldn't think it necessary."

Meurant's excitement had subsided. He listened vaguely to what was being said, as if it were of no concern to him. Mostly he stared at the swirling waters of the Marne, downstream.

Lapointe went on with his explanation:

"While he was rowing, the man who was in the boat had his back turned to the bank. So he couldn't see Meurant, who was standing near this tree."

"Did you know he was going to shoot?"

"I didn't know he was armed."

Maigret's face remained impassive. Yet Janvier cast him a quick glance, as if he had suddenly begun to understand.

"The bow of the boat touched the bank. The rower stood up, seized the painter, and as he turned around he found himself face to face with Meurant, who was hardly three yards away from him.

"I can't say whether they exchanged words or not. I was too far away.

"Almost immediately, Meurant drew a revolver from his pocket and stretched out his right arm.

"The other man, standing ready to get out, must have been hit by the two bullets, shot one after the other. He let go of the painter. His hands beat the air, and he fell into the water headfirst. . . ."

Everybody was now looking at the water. The rain, during the last few days, had swollen the river, which had a yellowish color, and in certain places there were swirling eddies.

"I asked the innkeeper's wife to notify the police and I ran across to here. . . ."

"Were you armed?"

"No."

Lapointe added, perhaps unthinkingly:

"There was no danger."

The local police could not understand. Nor could the men from the Flying Squad. Even if they had read the newspaper reports of the trial, they were not aware of the details of the case.

"Meurant made no attempt to run away. He remained in the same spot, watching the corpse disappear, then reappear again two or three times, always a little farther on, until it sank altogether.

"When I reached his side, he dropped the gun. I didn't touch it."

The revolver was embedded in the mud of the lane beside a dead branch.

"He said nothing?"

"Two words only:

" 'It's over.' "

The struggle was indeed over now for Gaston Meurant. His body seemed flabbier, his face puffy with tiredness.

He did not look triumphant, felt no need to explain himself, to justify himself. It was entirely his own affair.

In his view he had done what he had to do.

Would he ever have found peace otherwise? Would he find it from now on?

The public prosecutor's men from Melun would soon be arriving on the spot. The madwoman, on her threshold, was still nodding her head, never having seen so many people around her house before.

"It's quite likely," Maigret said to his colleagues,

"that you may make some discoveries when you go through the cottage."

He could have remained with them, helped in the search.

"Gentlemen, I shall send you all the information you will need."

He would not be taking Meurant back to Paris, since Meurant no longer belonged to the Quai des Orfèvres, or to the public prosecutor for the Seine district.

It would be in another law court, in Melun, that he would appear for the second time before the assizes.

Maigret asked Lapointe and Janvier:

"Are you coming, boys?"

He shook hands all around. Then, as he was turning away, he took his last look at Ginette's husband.

Suddenly conscious of his weariness, probably, the man had leaned against the tree again, and as he watched the chief inspector leave, there was a look almost of melancholy in his eyes.

Eight

Few words were exchanged during the drive back. Several times Lapointe opened his mouth, but Maigret's silence was so deep, so deliberate, that he did not dare say anything.

Janvier was driving and he had the feeling that, little by little, things were slipping into place.

But for the difference of a mile or two, they would have been taking Gaston Meurant back themselves.

"Perhaps it's just as well that way," murmured Janvier, as if he were speaking to himself.

Maigret did not approve or disapprove. To what, besides, had Janvier been alluding exactly?

The three of them climbed the staircase together at Police Headquarters, separated in the corridor, Lapointe and Janvier going into the duty room, while Maigret entered his office, where he hung his coat and hat in the closet.

He did not touch the bottle of brandy that he kept handy for some of his visitors. He had hardly had time to fill a pipe when Lucas knocked on the door and put in front of him a thick file.

"I found that upstairs, Chief. You might say it all hangs together."

And it did, in fact, all hang together. It was the file of a certain Pierre Millard, called Pierrot, thirty-two years old, born in Paris, in the Goutte-d'Or district.

He had had a police record since he was eighteen years old, when he appeared for the first time at the Seine police court, for procuring. Later he had two other convictions on the same count, with a period in Fresnes jail, then a conviction for assault and battery in Marseilles, and finally five years in the prison at Fontevrault, for breaking into a factory in Bordeaux and violent assault on a night watchman, who had been discovered half dead.

He was released from prison a year and a half ago. Since then, they had lost track of him.

Maigret lifted the receiver, called Toulon.

"Is that you, Blanc? Well, it's all over up here. Two bullets in the hide of a certain Pierre Millard, called Pierrot."

"A short, dark fellow?"

"Yes. They are busy searching for his body in the Marne, where he fell in headfirst. Does the name mean anything to you?"

"I'd have to have a word with my men about it. I seem to remember that he was prowling around here a little more than a year ago."

"That's more than likely. He came out of Fontevrault about then and was therefore prohibited from staying here. Since you've now got his name, could you perhaps put a few definite questions to Alfred Meurant? Is he still with you?"

"Yes. Do you want me to call you back?"

"Yes, please."

In Paris, at any rate, Millard had been prudent. Though he probably came frequently, almost every day, he was careful not to spend the night there. He had found a safe refuge beside the Marne, in the cottage belonging to the old woman, who was probably his grandmother.

He had not budged since the double murder on Rue Manuel. Ginette Meurant had made no attempt to visit him. She had not sent him any message. She was probably kept in the dark about his hiding place.

If things had happened differently, if Nicolas Cajou, in particular, had not given his evidence, Gaston Meurant would have been condemned to death, or to forced labor for the rest of his life. At best, considering the slight doubt in his favor and his unblemished past, he might have got off with twenty years.

Whereas Millard, once the verdict had been brought, could have left his hole, gone to the provinces or abroad, where Ginette Meurant could easily have joined him.

"Hello. Yes . . ."

They were calling him from Seine-et-Marne. The Flying Squad at Gournay informed him that they had discovered the gold pieces, the bearer bonds, and a certain number of bank notes in an old wallet.

The whole lot had been buried, in a can, in the geese and ducks' pen.

They had not yet fished out the body, which they hoped to find, like most bodies drowned in that reach, at the Chelles weir, where the lockkeeper was quite accustomed to it.

They had made some other discoveries in the old woman's house, among them, in the loft, an ancient trunk containing a Second Empire wedding dress, a suit, other dresses, some made of puce or pale-blue silk, embroidered and with yellowed lace. The most unexpected find was a Zouave's uniform from the beginning of the century.

Mother Goose could scarcely remember anything about her family, and the death of her grandson didn't seem to have affected her. When they had spoken of taking her to Gournay for questioning, she was concerned only about her birds, and they had had to promise to bring her back the same evening.

They would hardly bother about her past, or her children, of whom no trace could be found.

She would probably still live for years in her cottage by the waterside.

"Janvier!"

"Yes, Chief."

"Will you take Lapointe with you and go to Rue Delambre?"

"Am I to bring her here?"

"Yes."

"You don't think I ought to take a warrant with me?"

Maigret, as an officer of Paris Police Headquarters, was empowered to sign an order to appear and he did it on the spot.

"What if she asks any questions?"

"Say nothing."

"Shall I handcuff her?"

"Only if it's absolutely necessary."

Blanc called back from Toulon.

"I've just been asking some interesting questions."

"Did you tell him of Millard's death?"

"Of course."

"Did he seem surprised?"

"No. He didn't even bother to pretend."

"Did he come clean?"

"More or less. That's up to you to judge. He was careful not to say anything that might incriminate himself. He admits that he knew Millard. He met him several times, more than seven years ago, in Paris and Marseilles. Then Millard got five years, and Alfred Meurant heard nothing from him.

"When he got out of Fontevrault, Millard came back to hang around Marseilles, then Toulon. He was pretty down on his luck and was trying to get back in the game. His plan, according to Meurant, was not to do the odd job anymore, but to bring off something big that would set him up once and for all.

"As soon as he'd refurbished his wardrobe, he was intending to return to Paris.

"He stayed only a few weeks on the coast. Meurant admits that he gave him small sums, that he introduced him to his friends, and that they helped him also.

"As for Ginette Meurant, her brother-in-law talks of her jokingly. He apparently said to Millard, just as he was leaving:

" 'If you're ever short of a woman, there's always my little sister-in-law; she's married to an imbecile and she's pretty bored.'

"He swears that was all. He gave him Ginette's address and also told him that she liked going to a dance hall on Rue des Gravilliers.

"If you can believe him, he heard no further news of Pierre Millard, or of Ginette either."

This was not necessarily true, but it was plausible.
"What shall I do with him?"

"Get a statement from him and release him. But don't let him out of your sight, because we'll need him for the trial."

If there was a trial! New investigations would begin as soon as Lapointe and Janvier brought Ginette Meurant into Maigret's office.

Would they be able to establish with sufficient certainty her complicity with her lover?

Nicolas Cajou would go to identify Millard's body, then the chambermaid, and others as well.

Afterward, there would be the preliminary examination, then, eventually, the file would be referred to the grand jury.

During all that time it was more than probable that Ginette would remain in prison.

Then, one day, she would appear at the assizes in her turn.

Maigret would be summoned as a witness once more. The jury would try to understand something of this story that had taken place in a world so different from their own familiar universe.

Before that, since the case was more straightforward and the docket was not so full at the Seine-et-Marne assizes, Maigret would be summoned to Melun.

With other witnesses he would be shut up in a gloomy, hushed room resembling a sacristy, where he would await his turn, watching the door and listening to the dull echoes from the courtroom.

He would see Gaston Meurant again between two policemen, would swear to tell the truth, the whole truth, nothing but the truth.

Would he really tell the whole truth? Hadn't there been one particular moment, while the telephone was ringing incessantly in his office, where he kept some control on all the characters, when he had accepted a responsibility that was hard to explain away?

Might he not have been able to . . . ?

In two years he would no longer have to worry about other people's problems. He would be living with Madame Maigret, far from the Quai des Orfèvres and the courts where men are judged, in an old house like a rectory, and for hours on end he would sit in a punt moored to some stakes, watching the water flow past, fishing.

His office was full of his pipe smoke. Next door he could hear typewriters tapping away, telephones ringing.

He gave a start when there came a light tap on the door and it opened to reveal Lapointe's young figure.

Had he really jerked back guiltily, as if somebody were coming to call him to account?

"She's here, Chief. Do you want to see her right away?"

And Lapointe waited, seeing clearly that Maigret was slowly coming to from a dream—or a nightmare.

Noland
23 November 1959

By the year 2000, 2 out of 3 Americans could be illiterate.

It's true.

Today, 75 million adults...about one American in three, can't read adequately. And by the year 2000, U.S. News & World Report envisions an America with a literacy rate of only 30%.

Before that America comes to be, you can stop it...by joining the fight against illiteracy today.

Call the Coalition for Literacy at toll-free **1-800-228-8813** and volunteer.

**Volunteer
Against Illiteracy.
The only degree you need
is a degree of caring.**

Ad Council Coalition for Literacy